**"Hurry, Rachel. The fire is spreading over the roof."**

The sound of his voice calmed the fear rising in her even as she climbed to the window and grabbed Jake's hands to hold tight. With her arms hanging out the window and her upper chest lying on the bottom of it, her legs dangled in midair in the bathroom. She tried to move forward, but something sharp scraped her side.

"There must be some glass on my right, but don't stop."

"Sorry, I thought I got all the glass out of the frame."

Another crash sounded behind her. Time was running out.

Rachel managed to shift a bit while Jake said, "I'll be right back. I remember there was a blanket in the shed." Jake raced toward the small building.

The scent of smoke and burning wood bombarded Rachel. Someone wanted to destroy the house and Rachel and her aunt with it. But why? Coughs racked her while Jake rushed back. He took the blanket and put it between her and the window frame.

"This should help you move easier." Then he grabbed her arms and yanked.

"Just get me out." She imagined the flames eating away at the door and any second bursting into the room...

**Margaret Daley**, an award-winning author of ninety books (five million sold worldwide), has been married for over forty years and is a firm believer in romance and love. When she isn't traveling, she's writing love stories, often with a suspense thread, and corralling her three cats, who think they rule her household. To find out more about Margaret, visit her website at margaretdaley.com.

**Books by Margaret Daley**

**Love Inspired Suspense**

***Alaskan Search and Rescue***

*The Yuletide Rescue*
*To Save Her Child*
*The Protector's Mission*
*Standoff at Christmas*

***Capitol K-9 Unit***

*Security Breach*

***Guardians, Inc.***

*Christmas Bodyguard*
*Protecting Her Own*
*Hidden in the Everglades*
*Christmas Stalking*
*Guarding the Witness*
*Bodyguard Reunion*

Visit the Author Profile page at Harlequin.com for more titles.

# STANDOFF AT CHRISTMAS

MARGARET DALEY

HARLEQUIN® LOVE INSPIRED® SUSPENSE

Recycling programs for this product may not exist in your area.

ISBN-13: 978-0-373-67720-7

Standoff at Christmas



This edition published by arrangement with Love Inspired Books.



www.Harlequin.com

**Printed in U.S.A.**

Who gave Himself for our sins, that He might deliver us from this present evil world, according to the will of God and our Father.

—*Galatians* 1:4

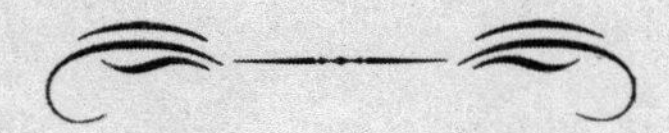

For Helen, who introduced me to Alaska

# ONE

Rachel Hart left the warmth of her office building to trudge through the snow toward the processing center at the Port Aurora Fishery. The lights on in the building beckoned her in the predawn morning. The sun was just rising to the east in Port Aurora, Alaska, and then it would set by three in the afternoon.

She was used to the winters, having lived most of her twenty-eight years in the town, but today she wished the sun would shine for more than six hours. She looked up at the dark clouds rolling in and quickened her pace. An omen?

She lifted her cell phone and listened again to the message from Aunt Betty. "Rachel, I've got to talk to you. Today. Alone. Something's wrong. I don't know what to do. I'm taking my break at nine this morning." Luckily, today was payday, so Rachel could use her position as bookkeeper as an excuse to visit the processing center.

The urgency in her aunt's voice shivered down Rachel's spine. *What's wrong? Aunt Betty is always so cheerful and calm.* She must have called earlier while Rachel was away from her office.

Entering the building, Rachel walked down the hallway that led to the mail room for the employees who worked in the processing center. It was part of the large break room next to the office where Sean O'Hara managed this part of the company.

When she popped into the break room, Aunt Betty sat at the table with one of the newer employees. "I've got your paychecks." Rachel covered the distance to the two women and handed Betty and Ingrid their checks. "The next one will come with a bonus right before we close down for Christmas." She wanted to pull her aunt out in the hallway and find out what was wrong, but when she looked at the older woman with touches of gray hair around her face, her brown eyes widened and she shook her head slightly.

"I'm just thankful for the extra hours." Aunt Betty opened the envelope, looked at the amount and forced a grin, the corners of her mouth twitching.

In past years the fishery had closed down during the winter months, and the crabs were sent to another plant. Rachel had been thrilled about that part of the fishery's expansion in the last year. So had everyone else, especially Aunt Betty.

"But I'm also excited to have a few weeks off for the holidays." Her hand shaking, Aunt Betty stuck her paycheck in her pocket.

Rachel wanted to ask the other employee to leave but swallowed those words and instead said, "Me, too. Jake Nichols got in late last night for the holidays." She should be excited, but a lot had happened between them since they were teenagers. Jake had been her best friend while growing up, but when he left town eight years ago, they lost touch.

"I know Lawrence is glad to see Jake here, especially after what happened in Anchorage in August." Aunt Betty finished off her coffee.

"What happened?" Ingrid asked, having only recently been hired.

Rachel moved to the mailboxes and began stuffing the envelopes into them, hoping Ingrid left soon. "There was a serial bomber. Jake, a K-9 officer in Anchorage, was working one of the crime sites, searching for survivors or missing people, when the building collapsed on him. He nearly died." And he had made it clear he didn't want her to come see him while he was recovering. That hurt—still did.

Ingrid hugged her arms. "Oh my. Search and rescue is dangerous, but I'm finding out it's even more so here in Alaska with so much wilderness."

"Where are you from?" Rachel asked as she finished her task.

"Seattle."

"That's where Brad Howard's new partner is from."

"Who?"

Rachel paused at the exit. "Peter Rodin. Have you heard of him?"

"He was on the news from time to time," Ingrid said.

Aunt Betty's eyebrows rose. "About what?"

"His foundation gives money to various projects for the city." Ingrid rose and headed toward Rachel. "My break is over."

Relieved the woman was leaving, she moved to the side to let Ingrid pass, while her aunt's expression morphed into the apprehensive look she'd worn when Rachel first came into the break room.

When Aunt Betty remained in her seat, Ingrid said from the hallway, "Aren't you going back to work?"

Her aunt blinked several times. "Yes, I just want Rachel to pass a message on to my sister about this weekend."

Ingrid started toward the end of the hallway but much slower than her usual brisk pace.

As soon as Ingrid turned the corner and disappeared, Rachel moved toward her aunt. "What's going on? I got your message."

Waving to Rachel to come closer, Betty pushed to her feet. "I'm glad Jake is home. He's a police officer. He might know what's going on and help. I need some…" Her aunt's voice faded into the silence.

Rachel heard footsteps and glanced toward the door. Sean O'Hara came into the break room.

"Hello, ladies." Sean's eyes brightened as they took in Rachel. "Ah, payday. That's always a good day around here."

"Yes, it is. I need to get back to work." As a pallor crossed her features, Aunt Betty took her paper cup, crushed it and tossed it into the trash can by the door as she left.

Her concern growing, Rachel watched her leave as though a grizzly bear was hot on her tail. This wasn't like her aunt. What did she want with Jake? What had her scared? She'd get in touch with her later. Maybe she would swing by her house on the way home today. Aunt Betty only lived a mile away from Aunt Linda's, the older of her two aunts, and the one she lived with.

"I saw Jake down the hall. I told him I'd give him the grand tour. I know you two were good friends growing up. You're welcome to come along."

"Jake is here?" He and Sean had been friends in high school, too, so it wasn't that odd.

"Yeah, he couldn't believe all the changes around here. He wants to see the new vessels, processing center and shipping warehouse."

Rachel couldn't shake the worried expression on Aunt Betty's face. This might be her chance to see if she could talk to her on the floor, rather than wait until later. "Make it the short tour. I need to get back to work. Everyone will want their checks."

"I just came inside. It started snowing."

"Right on time, for a change."

Sean chuckled. "Predicting the weather isn't an exact science. But I'll be glad to get home before the hard stuff hits, which shouldn't be until tonight."

Jake Nichols turned as they approached him at the entrance into the large processing room. She took in his tall, muscular build, blue eyes and short black hair—the same and yet something had changed in the last couple of years since she'd visited Anchorage. It had to be the accident that nearly took his life in August.

Jake's look warmed when he saw her. Maybe in the next month they would be able to renew their friendship, and he would come back to Port Aurora more frequently.

"Rachel was in the break room. She thought she would join us like old times." Sean opened the wide double doors into the cavernous space where the fish and shellfish were processed for shipping to the rest of the United States.

Sean began pointing out some of the additional machines and the areas that were expanded this year. Rachel stepped away and glimpsed Aunt Betty decked out in her protective clothing with white hat and long gloves at the end of a conveyor belt. While Sean strolled with Jake to various stations, Rachel hurried toward her aunt. Out of the corner of her eye, Rachel spied Ingrid approaching Aunt Betty. Her aunt locked eyes with Rachel and shook her head. She came to a halt. Suddenly, she felt like she was in the middle of a spy movie, which was ridiculous. Aunt Betty could be melodramatic at times, but usually she was levelheaded.

Ingrid paused next to her aunt and said something. Aunt Betty nodded. Rachel would have to wait to appease her curiosity. She released a long breath and pivoted, searching for Jake and Sean.

She caught up with them near the freezers. "I need to get back to headquarters. It was great seeing you again, Jake. You and your grandfather are supposed to come to dinner tonight. A welcome-home party."

"I'll come with you." Jake slanted his glance briefly toward Aunt Betty.

Did he see that nonverbal exchange between her aunt and her? Jake had always been perceptive, which probably made him a good police officer. Rachel gave Jake a smile, waiting until he shook hands with Sean and joined her before heading out of the processing room. In the hallway leading to the exit, she asked, "What do you think of the new additions to the fishery?"

"Impressive what has been done in a short time. Gramps told me things were automated and upgraded where they could be. What's in the building next to this one? That's new."

"The shipping warehouse. Everything going by boat to Anchorage is loaded easily when the vessel docks right outside. They even dredged the harbor to allow for bigger ships."

"How much is flown out?"

"Maybe a third—more in the warmer months. Ready?" She peered at Jake as he reached to open the main door. His strong profile had been shaped by the recent events in his life—the lines sharper, adding a hard edge to his features.

His hand on the knob, he peered sideways at her. For a few seconds his gaze trapped hers, and she didn't want to look away.

"Is something wrong with your aunt?"

"I don't know. She called upset, but we haven't had a chance to talk alone yet. I'll stop by after work to see what's going on."

"When she went into the processing room, I said hi to her and she didn't even acknowledge it. She just kept going. I know I've been gone, but that's not like her. She's the first to want to know everything about a person."

"I agree she isn't acting normal." Rachel headed into the lightly falling snow and made her way toward the office building.

She'd make sure Aunt Betty came to dinner. She'd been invited. The storm shouldn't hit full force until after midnight, and if she had to, Aunt Betty could stay at her sister's.

"Why were you at the processing center? I was surprised to see you there."

Jake smiled. "To see you. I saw you entering the building and came to say hi. I hear you were promoted to bookkeeper."

"Yes, which reminds me, I have to finish my rounds and give out the payroll checks. I'll see you tonight."

Midway through the afternoon, Rachel called Sean's office to see if she could talk with Aunt Betty. His secretary told her that her aunt had clocked out early and gone home. Rachel tried Aunt Betty's home number. No answer. She might not be home yet.

When Rachel was ready to leave two hours later, she made the call to her aunt's again, and the phone still rang and rang. Rachel's worry mounted. What if she was sick and couldn't answer it? She had looked pale earlier. And why had she wanted Jake's help?

Rachel hurried to her Jeep and navigated the snow-packed streets to the outskirts of Port Aurora. Aunt Betty's house was on the same road out of town but before Aunt Linda's house. Both her aunts and Lawrence Nichols, Jake's grandfather, loved living a little out from town.

When she reached Aunt Betty's drive, she drove down it and parked in front of the cabin, not far from the shed where her aunt's truck was. She was home.

Rachel made her way to the covered front porch, the wind beginning to pick up and blow the snow around as it fell. Rachel knocked. A minute later she did again.

When Betty didn't come to answer the door, Rachel stepped to the side and peeked into the living room window. She froze at the sight of the chaos inside.

Jake finished getting the supplies for Gramps and strolled toward the checkout at the Port Aurora General Store. It had been good to see Rachel again. Talking to her this morning made him realize he missed their conversations. While in Anchorage, he'd kept himself busy, and he'd let their friendship slip. He should have come back to town before this. Port Aurora had been his home for years until… He shook the image of Celeste from his thoughts and put the items on the counter. Marge, the owner's wife, began ringing up his purchases.

A bell rang, announcing yet another customer coming into the popular store near the harbor. Jake glanced toward the person entering. He stiffened. He'd known he would see Celeste Howard—the woman who broke off their engagement eight years ago—during his extended stay at Gramps's, but he'd hoped not the first day in town.

Their gazes clashed. He gritted his teeth and swiveled his attention to Marge to pay for his supplies.

Marge's eyes twinkled. "She always comes in right before Brad leaves work and gets a drink at the café. She usually picks him up." Marge, one of the best gossipers in Port Aurora, waited for his response.

He smiled and said, "Thanks. Merry Christmas," then grabbed his bag and started for the exit of the store, which was dripping with Christmas decorations.

Celeste intercepted his departure. "Hi, Jake. It's good to see you again. I heard about your injury. How are you?"

She had meant everything to him at one time, but when he looked at her now, a cold rock hardened in his gut. "I'm fine, as you can see." Then he continued his trek toward the door, welcoming the blast of icy wind as he stepped onto the porch.

"Yes. Five or six hours from now they might not be."

"If the storm blows through quickly, they'll have the roads plowed by tomorrow afternoon."

"All the way out here?" They didn't when he lived here as a child, but Port Aurora's population had been only twenty-eight hundred in the winter. With its growth came more needs for the residents.

"Yep, that's called progress. They don't plow the long drive, but I'll get out there and do that tomorrow morning."

"I can."

"No, you're on vacation."

"I've been on vacation for months, and frankly I can't wait to get back to work."

Gramps turned and ambled toward the great room where he spent a lot of his time. "Then let's pray your doctor says you're ready to go back to work at the first of January. Did you see any old friends?"

"Rachel and Sean." Since Celeste wasn't a friend, he left her name out. Whenever she was mentioned, Gramps always got angry.

"How's Rachel?"

"Fine." Jake sat on the couch while his grandfather took his place in his special lounger. "We really didn't talk long. Aunt Betty was upset about something, and Rachel was focused on that."

"Really? Betty is one lady that goes with the flow. She doesn't let much of anything get to her. I should learn something from her."

The landline rang, and Jake reached toward the end table and snatched up the receiver. "Hello."

"Jake, I'm so glad you're home." The relief in Rachel's voice came through loud and clear.

"What's wrong?"

"I stopped by Aunt Betty's house on the way home, and no one answered the door, but her car is here. I just looked into the living room window and someone has tossed her place. It's a mess."

"Call the police, stay outside and I'll be right there."

"I'm already inside. My cell doesn't work this far from town. The first thing I did was call you."

"Make the call to the police and then get out. Okay?"

"Yes." The urgency in Jake's voice heightened her concern for her aunt.

# TWO

After reporting to the police about the trashed living room, Rachel hung up her aunt's phone not far from the front door and started edging back. Her heart pounded against her rib cage, her breathing shallow. She should get out like Jake said, but what if Aunt Betty was knocked out on the floor? She didn't think an intruder was still there since there was no sign of a vehicle other than Aunt Betty's. But if someone robbed her, and from the disarray of drawers emptied and cushions tossed on the floor, it was obvious that was what happened, then her aunt could be hurt, tied up or even…

No, she wouldn't consider that. She wouldn't leave until she found her aunt. The least she could do until Jake came was walk through her cabin and search. Rachel had first-aid training because of all the hiking and camping she did in the warmer months. If Aunt Betty was hurt, she might need medical attention right away.

She moved through the clutter, careful not to step on anything. Maybe this was the only room involved. Maybe her aunt had been looking for something in the living room and…

When Rachel entered the kitchen, it was worse. Everything was out of the cabinets and refrigerator. If someone had been looking for something, they probably found it, but Aunt Betty had little in the way of money. Rachel noticed the television was still in place as well as the small appliances. There was a walk-in pantry near the arctic entry at the back. The wooden floors were littered with flour, sugar, cereal. She would disturb the kitchen if she walked across it. Instead, she'd check the rest of the house first. By then, she hoped that Jake had arrived, and he would know how to proceed.

She walked several feet into her aunt's bedroom before she couldn't go any farther because of the mess on the floor, but from that point she could look into the open closet. No Aunt Betty.

A sound from the living room sent a wave of panic through her. It was probably Jake, but just in case, she flattened herself behind the open door.

"Rachel, where are you?"

Jake's deep baritone voice pushed the panic away, and she came out from behind the bedroom door. "I'm in Aunt Betty's bedroom."

"I should have known you wouldn't listen to me," Jake mumbled as he came into the short hallway.

"You brought Mitch." Rachel knelt next to the leashed German shepherd and petted him. "He looks good."

"I thought if we needed to search for your aunt he could help. He loves tracking. Have you found anything?"

"A mess, as you can see for yourself, but no sign of Aunt Betty. I haven't looked in the bathroom or the second bedroom, though."

"I'll check them and then we'll wait for the police. You stay here with Mitch. This will only take a minute." After handing her the German shepherd's leash, Jake walked toward the open bathroom door and peered inside. "The same thing here but no Betty."

The door to the second bedroom was ajar but not open. Jake shouldered his way into the room but stayed by the entrance. "She must not be here. Could she have gone somewhere with anyone?"

"Maybe. I suppose she could have fled when she saw the chaos, but she most likely would have contacted her sister or me."

"Have you called Linda?"

"No, I didn't want to alarm her if I didn't have to. If anything happened to Aunt Betty, we would be devastated." Like when Jake had left Port Aurora years ago. His departure had stunned her, as if he'd taken part of her with him. She cared about the town and its people, but her family and Jake had been the most important people in her life. "I'll call her, then we can stay inside by the front door."

While Rachel placed a call to Aunt Linda, Jake picked his way through the mess in the living room to look into the kitchen. When she answered, Rachel said, "I'm at Aunt Betty's house. Her car is here, but she isn't. She was upset today, and I wanted to make sure she was all right. Do you know anything?"

"Well, that explains the weird message from her at lunchtime. I was waiting until she got home to call her. Her car is there?"

"Yes, where she parks it in the shed." Rachel glanced at the chaos and hated to tell Aunt Linda, but she continued. "Someone tore her house apart as though they were looking for something. For all I know, they could have found it."

Her aunt gasped. "I'll be right there."

"No, stay put. The police are on the way. What did the message say?"

"That she should never have taken those pictures."

"What pictures?" Rachel asked as Jake returned to her side.

"I'm not sure. You know how she's always snapping pictures. She was excited about some new project and was going to show us this weekend. She told me one day the town might want to even display the photos."

Maybe that had been what she'd wanted to talk to Rachel about. But then if that were the case, why had someone searched her house? Strange. "Display what?"

"She was being secretive. You know how she is about the big reveal when she gets an idea. Why would anyone try to steal from her? The only things worth taking are the TV and her camera, although it isn't a digital one like most people use today. Are they still there?"

"The TV is. I didn't check for the camera in her darkroom, but Jake said that second bedroom was trashed like the rest of the house."

"Really, I can't see someone taking it. It's old. Not something that someone would steal. How about her food processor I gave her for her birthday?"

Rachel remembered seeing it in the kitchen, in pieces. "It's here."

A long pause from her aunt, then in a tight, low tone, she said, "Then something has happened to her." Her voice sounded thick.

Rachel peered out the front window, seeing headlights piercing the snowy darkness. "The police have arrived. I've got to go. I'll be home as soon as I can. We're probably overreacting." At least she prayed she was.

"Rachel, let me know what's going on. If you need my help, call. Are you sure I shouldn't come over?"

"Yes, she might call you. Someone needs to be there. Besides, the police are here, and they'll probably kick us out while they check the house. When we find Aunt Betty, she'll need you and me to help her clean this mess up." *If they find Aunt Betty.* She couldn't rid her mind of that thought.

Jake opened the door for the two police officers from town—the older man, Police Chief Randall Quay, and the younger one, Officer Steve Bates.

The chief shook Jake's hand. "It's good to see you back home. What do you think?" He gestured toward the trashed living room.

"I've searched the house as much as I could without disturbing anything, but there are some places I didn't get to check. The closet in the second bedroom, the pantry and the back arctic entry."

"Aunt Betty used the closet in the second bedroom as a darkroom."

The chief nodded once, then turned back to Jake. "Can you help me? Since you're here, I'd like to send Officer Bates on up the road. We are shorthanded with this storm that moved in early. It seems to bring the crazies out."

"Sure, I can help. Mitch here can track if we need that."

"Betty is a special lady. She taught me in Sunday school." Chief Quay moved farther into the room while his officer left. He frowned, his gaze fixed on a broken vase. "She didn't deserve this." He pulled out a camera and started taking pictures of the living room.

"I can cover the kitchen." Jake started forward.

"I appreciate it. We need to find Betty." The chief turned to Rachel. "Can you make some calls to people she may know and see if she's with them?"

"I already called Aunt Linda, and she's not with her. But I know a few others she's close with at the fishery. I'll give them a call." Rachel pulled out her cell to use the list of phone numbers stored in it. She was relieved to be able to help and needed to stay busy to keep from fixating on what might have happened to her aunt. She picked up the phone and began dialing.

Jake carefully started on one side of the kitchen and made his way around it. Behind the island in the center in the midst of the emptied flour on the floor, he found footprints—one set, too big to be Betty's, more like a man's size eleven. He took a photo with his cell of that and anything else of interest. He refrained from touching anything in case the chief wanted to dust for latent prints.

So far no evidence that Betty had been here when this happened—except her car parked in the shed. That would need to be searched, too. In fact, after he went through the kitchen he would go out the back arctic entry and check Betty's old pickup.

When he reached the pantry, he used a

gloved hand to open the door. His gaze riveted to the spots of blood on the wooden floor about six inches inside. He lifted his eyes and scanned the disarray, homing in on bloody fingerprints on a shelf as if someone tried to hold on to it. Maybe trying to get up? Whatever went on in here, a fight occurred in this walk-in pantry. Did the intruder find Betty hiding?

The question still persisted. *Then where is Betty?*

He took more photos, then proceeded to the arctic entry. A pair of boots and a woman's heavy coat hanging on a peg were the only things in the small room. He took the coat and let Mitch sniff it, then kept hold of it in case he needed it again. His dog smelled the floor and paused by the exit outside. This was probably the way Betty came into her house since this was closer than the front entrance to the shed. Jake returned to the kitchen and grabbed a flashlight on the wall by the door.

On the stoop, Jake took in the area. The snow falling had filled in any footsteps, but that wouldn't stop Mitch. His German shepherd sniffed the air and started down the three steps, then headed toward Betty's pickup.

As he approached the driver side of the vehicle, he spied a bloody print on the metal handle. Not a good sign. Mitch barked at the door.

Jake said, “Stay,” then skirted the rear of the old truck and opened the passenger door. The seat was empty.

Then he investigated under the tarp over the bed of the Ford F-150, using the interior light from the cab. Nothing.

“Where is she?” Rachel asked as she approached, carrying a flashlight. “I called at least twenty women she knew from church and the fishery, and no one knows where she is. One lady said she got ill after lunch and left. That would mean she should have gotten home by one. What happened in those three hours?”

*Something not good.*

“Is the chief through in the house?”

“He didn’t find anything in the second bedroom but was going to go through Betty’s. Did you find anything?”

He hated to tell her. Rachel had always been close to both of her aunts. “Blood in the pantry and on the driver’s door handle.”

“Do you think someone attacked her in the house and—” Rachel swallowed hard “—somehow she got away? Did she try to leave and that person caught up with her?” Her large brown eyes shone with unshed tears.

"I didn't see any blood inside on the seat. I don't think she ever opened the door."

Rachel blinked once, and a tear ran down her face. She swung around in a full circle, the flashlight sending an arc of illumination across the yard. "Then where is she? Why would anyone want to hurt Aunt Betty?"

Jake moved to his dog and let him inhale her scent on the coat again. "Find." While Mitch smelled around, Jake said to Rachel, "Let's see if he can pick up a trail going away from the house or shed."

Blond hair peeking out from under her beanie, Rachel swept her arm to indicate the yard outside the shed. "She could have decided to hide out here because she didn't have her truck keys on her."

"Maybe."

"But then why didn't she come forward when we arrived?" Rachel took one look at his sober expression and added, "Never mind. She would if she could..." Her gaze locked with his. "Could have."

Mitch picked up a scent, barked, then headed out of the shed across the field toward a stand of spruce and other evergreens. Giving his dog a long leash, Jake followed with Rachel beside him. Mitch plowed his way through four or five inches of snow.

At a place his German shepherd had disturbed, Jake yelled, “Halt,” then stooped to examine a couple of drops of blood in the white snow with his flashlight.

Rachel’s gasp sounded above the noise of the wind. He glanced over his shoulder at her face, white like the snow. He wished he could erase the fear in her eyes.

“You should return to the house and let the chief know.”

Rachel shook her head. “I started this. I want to find her. I’ve been praying she’s still alive and only hurt. Time is of the essence. She could freeze to death.”

He rose, commanded Mitch to continue his search, then took her gloved hand in his. “We’ll do this together.” He felt better having her by his side rather than trekking back to the house alone about five hundred yards away.

As they trailed behind Mitch, Jake prepared himself. Betty could have been out here without a coat for hours. He stopped again a couple of times when more blood became visible in the glow of his light. Mitch was following Betty’s path closely. If anyone could find her, his dog could.

Among the trees, the snow on the ground wasn't as thick because the top branches were heavy with it. They saw evidence of more blood, and Rachel's expression lost all hope her aunt was still alive. Tears returned to glisten in her eyes.

Mitch's bark echoed through the woods. He stopped about twenty feet away. Jake spotted a shadowy lump in the snow and blocked Rachel's path. "Go back and get Chief Quay."

Rachel tried to look around Jake.

"Please, Rachel. I think Mitch found Betty."

"Then I need to see if I can help her."

"If she's alive, I can. I trained as a paramedic when I first went to Anchorage." He'd been debating whether to continue his career of being a police officer in the big city or wanting to try something else before making that decision.

She looked into his face, snowflakes catching on her long eyelashes. She blinked, trying to conquer the tears welling in her eyes.

"Please, Rachel."

She whirled about and hurried back, following the path already cut. When she'd cleared the trees, Jake quickened his pace toward Mitch. Betty, stiff as if totally frozen with a bloodied head wound, leaned against a tree trunk facing away from the house. Had she been trying to hide? Her lower body was covered with a white blanket of snow while she hugged her sweater-clad arms to her chest. She stared off into space.

Betty was dead, but Jake knelt next to her and felt for a pulse to make sure. He said a silent prayer, something he hadn't done in a long while. She was with the Lord.

He would find whoever did this.

# THREE

"Aunt Linda, I can call Lawrence and Jake and reschedule this dinner for another night." Rachel stood in the entrance to the kitchen where her aunt was cooking a beef stew and putting some rolls in the oven to bake.

"All I have to do is the bread. The stew has been simmering half the day." She turned from the stove, her eyes red from crying for the past hour. Aunt Linda held the baking sheet in her hands like a shield, her fingertips red from her tight grip on it. "I know Randall asked you to come home, but Jake stayed and I want to know what they found out about Betty's death. Murder! I still can't believe it." She slammed the cookie sheet on the countertop and placed the rolls on it. "My sister was one of the sweetest people in Port Aurora. She never hurt a soul. I've got to make some sense out of this."

"I don't know if we'll ever be able to do that."

"They should have been here five minutes ago. Call them to make sure they're coming," her aunt, a petite woman with short blond hair, said in a determined voice.

Aunt Linda was always where she was supposed to be on time, if not early. "I will," Rachel said before her aunt decided to do it instead. Since she'd returned home an hour ago, Aunt Linda had fluctuated between tears and anger, much like what Rachel had been experiencing since she glimpsed Aunt Betty leaning against the tree. Stiff. Snow covering her.

As Rachel made her way into the living room, she heard the doorbell. She continued into the arctic entry and let Jake and his grandfather into the house. They removed their snowshoes and stomped their feet to shake off what snow they could.

"You two walked?"

"The wind has died down some." Jake removed his beanie.

"But the snow is still coming down a lot." Rachel had been looking forward to seeing him and spending time with her best friend from childhood. A few months ago, he'd almost died, and now her aunt had been murdered.

"With what happened this afternoon, I

needed to walk some of my stress off." Jake hung his coat and his grandfather's on two pegs in the arctic entry and headed into the living room.

Lawrence looked around. "Where's Linda?"

"In the kitchen. Dinner will be soon."

"I'll go see how she's coping. I still can't believe someone would kill Betty." Lawrence strode from the room.

The second he was gone, Rachel pivoted toward Jake. "Tell me what happened after I left."

"How's Linda doing?"

"Mad one minute, emotional the next. She wants to find the person responsible and..." Rachel's mouth twisted. "I'm not sure what she would do, but she wants the murderer caught. She's trying to make some sense of what happened to her sister."

"Have her come in here, and I'll tell both of you before dinner. Although I can't say any of it makes sense."

Rachel headed toward the kitchen, but Lawrence and Aunt Linda were already at the doorway.

"I turned the oven on to warm so the rolls ought to be fine while Jake tells us what happened." Aunt Linda took a seat on the couch with Lawrence next to her, his arm around her shoulder. Her aunt leaned against Jake's grandfather as though she couldn't hold herself upright without him.

Jake stood by the roaring fireplace, while Rachel sat down and told her part of the story. "When I went back to Betty's house, Officer Bates had returned and was trying to pull fingerprints while the chief finished with photos, especially of the kitchen and pantry. When I told him what we found, he left his officer processing evidence and told me to go home, then he started toward the woods." The sight of Aunt Betty on the ground haunted her. Rachel shut the memory down and shifted her attention to Jake. "Your turn."

With his hands behind his back, he drew in a deep breath. "The chief took photos of Betty, then we carried her to the house. When I left, he was waiting for Doc to come take her. It appeared she died either from the head wound from someone hitting her with some kind of round object—possibly a can from the pantry—or she succumbed to the cold. Either way, the police chief is looking at the case as a murder."

Aunt Linda dropped her head, tears falling on her lap. "I can't believe this."

Lawrence cupped Aunt Linda's hand in her lap. "We haven't had a murder here in years. A couple of deadly bar fights. That's all."

"Do you know if they found what they were looking for?" Aunt Linda lifted her gaze, her eyes red.

"No. The police don't know what she had of value at her house." Jake stepped away from the fire and took the last seat in the living room. "Was the TV the only thing of value that a robber would steal?"

Her aunt shook her head. "She had a few pieces of jewelry, but nothing to kill over, a state-of-the-art food processor and an old Kodak camera. Do you think Chief Quay would like for me to go through the house and see if I can find anything?"

"I'll call him tomorrow. It might help to know if that was the motive for the break-in. Knowing the motive might help find the killer."

Rachel remembered her brief encounters with Aunt Betty earlier that day. "I don't think it's a robbery. I think Aunt Betty discovered something that concerned her. She asked about talking to you, Jake, because you were a police officer in Anchorage. Aunt Linda, do you know of any place she uses for hiding valuable items? I can't think of any."

Her head lowered, Aunt Linda stared at her folded hands, the thumbs twirling around each other. "She had a cubbyhole in her kitchen. If you didn't know about it, you wouldn't see it. It's where the two cabinets form an L-shape near the sink. But it only can hide small objects. She kept her spare key to the truck in there. A diamond ring our mother passed on to her. I'm not sure what else."

"Then that should be checked." Rachel glanced at Jake, who nodded. "We can do that tomorrow."

Her teeth digging into her lower lip, Aunt Linda rose. "Since we're her only living relatives, it's our responsibility to see to her—" she swallowed several times "—belongings. Now, I'm going to set the table, and dinner will be in about ten minutes."

Lawrence also stood. "I'll help."

After they left the room, Jake leaned across the end table that separated their chairs and said in a low voice, "Is something going on between your aunt and my grandfather?"

"Good friends. That's all. Over the years, they've helped each other, and their friendship has grown. It kind of reminds me of us when we were kids. Not that I'm saying theirs is childish. Aunt Linda told me a few years ago that she'd had a wonderful marriage she would always cherish in her memory, but she didn't want to get married again."

"How about you? I thought by now you'd be married. You have so much to offer a man."

*But not you.* When they had been friends, before Celeste, Rachel had wondered if Jake and she would fall in love, and whether the marriage would work—unlike her mother's six marriages—because she knew Jake so well. Her mother would date a man for a couple of months, marry him, then discard him in a few years. "I don't have a lot of faith in marriage—at least what I've seen of it."

"You might be right. A successful marriage is becoming rarer."

"Is my cynicism rubbing off on you?"

He grinned. "I've been around you for a day, and look what happened." His gaze shifted to the Christmas tree in front of the living room window. "Your lights were what we focused on. Even with it snowing, we could see them from our front porch. Of course, it's not snowing as hard as earlier."

"We always decorate the day after Thanksgiving. Aunt Betty comes over..." Thinking about how her aunt died churned her stomach. She needed to forget the last few hours for a while or she wouldn't be able to help Aunt Linda. "Is Lawrence going to put a tree up this year? He usually doesn't because he visits you in Anchorage."

"He hasn't said. Maybe I should go cut one down like we used to, and then he'd have no choice. He always insists we do when he comes to visit, so turnaround is fair play. He's really a kid at heart."

Rachel took in the hard edge to Jake's expression and the reserve he didn't have as a teen. She missed who he'd been. "But you aren't. From what he's told me, you're very serious and focused."

"Being a police officer in a large town colors your perception. Sadly, I have covered murders. I'd forgotten the charm of Port Aurora and the lack of what I call *real crime.*"

"You should come home more often." This exchange brought memories of how they were as teenagers. They used to tell each other everything—until Celeste. She changed Jake. He became closed, and in the end he left because she married Brad Howard. That hurt her more than she cared to acknowledge.

"We'll see."

"Have you seen Celeste yet?"

His shoulders tensed. "I've only been here less than a day."

"But you were in town for hours, and it's a small place. She and Brad don't live far from the main street."

"I've seen that big house overlooking the harbor."

"You mean the audacious home looming over the town," she said with a forced chuckle.

Jake pushed to his feet. "I can smell the dinner, and I'm starving. Let's eat." He held out his hand to her.

Celeste was still a sore subject with him. That broke her heart. Rachel wanted him to be happy and move on from Celeste. Rachel placed her hand in his, and he tugged her up. For a few seconds they were only inches apart, his spicy scent—or maybe the Christmas tree nearby—teased her senses and blended with the aromas of the bread and beef stew.

*At least he loved someone once. You don't even want to take that chance.*

The next morning, after Gramps plowed the long drive from the road to the cluster of houses, Jake headed for town to talk with the police chief, a man he'd worked with for over a year, before he moved away. Randall had taught him a lot, but his real police training came when he went to Anchorage.

Jake parked in front of the police station, a small building, nothing like where he worked. When he entered, he saw the chief coming out of his office and putting a paper down in front of the dispatcher/secretary. From what he understood, only seven officers worked for the department besides Randall, three more than when he had been an officer on this force. That wasn't too bad in the winter months when the year-round population was a little over four thousand, but in the warmer months there was an influx of tourists, mostly hunters and fishermen.

Randall came toward Jake and shook his hand. "I'm sure glad you could help out yesterday. I have one officer on vacation, and with the storm yesterday, there are always more wrecks."

"While I'm here, I'd be glad to help out, if needed. I wanted to know what the cause of Betty's death was."

"The verdict was she passed out and froze to death. It was estimated by body temperature she was outside close to three hours."

"Are you calling it a murder?"

The chief nodded. "She wouldn't have been outside with a head wound if someone hadn't intruded in her house and hit her."

"Did you find the weapon?"

"Yes, a can of soup. I think the attacker left her in the pantry where she had probably been hiding and continued his search. She must have awakened and fled outside."

"How many people do you think it is?"

"We have two different sets of footprints in the house that weren't Betty's." Randall half leaned, half sat on his dispatcher's desk as Officers Bates and Clark walked from the back of the station, talking.

"Any latent prints that you could match?"

Randall signaled for Bates to join them. "Yes, one, but the print isn't in our system. Did Linda know what might have been taken from Betty's? If someone wanted to steal, I could think of many better off than her."

"No, but Linda and Rachel are going to start cleaning up since I checked with one of your officers this morning. He said you're through with the crime scene."

Randall glanced toward Bates. "We were there until late, processing the scene. Finished about ten o'clock. If Linda or Rachel find anything missing, please let me know."

Jake shifted slightly toward the young officer. "I'll leave you to talk business. I'm going by the general store for some cleaning supplies they might need at Betty's house, then to Port Aurora's Community Church. Linda couldn't get hold of the pastor this morning, so she wanted me to tell him Betty only wanted a small memorial service at church."

"That sounds like Betty, but it won't be small. I don't see how the church will be big enough for the service. She worked at the processing center at the fishery and was a moving force at church. I figure at least half the town will want to come." Randall reached behind him for a piece of paper and handed it to Bates. "Red Cunningham had his cell phone stolen. Check it out."

"Yes, sir. On it."

"Was Betty's cell on her?" Jake asked.

"From what I understand, she only had a landline at her house." Randall straightened. "I can't imagine not having a cell."

"Me, either. It's hard enough that it doesn't always work here." They nodded goodbye, and Jake left the police station and drove the half a mile to the general store, which was close to the harbor on the main street.

He decided to grab a cup of coffee, because

no one made it as good as Marge, then get the cleaning supplies. As he entered the store, his gaze almost immediately went to Brad and Celeste sitting at a table talking. Neither saw him, and he hoped it stayed that way.

He stood in line a couple of people behind Sean O'Hara. They had been in the same class in high school. If he had been spending time with Rachel growing up, usually Sean was with him. Sean placed his order, then turned away from the counter.

"I just heard about Betty this morning," Sean said when he glimpsed Jake. "She was such a good employee. I should have realized something was wrong when she went home early yesterday."

Jake moved up in the line. "Linda and Rachel are planning a memorial service for her next week. Police Chief Quay said the church wouldn't even be able to accommodate most of the people who would attend. If that's the case, is there anything at the fishery that could be used?"

Sean rubbed the back of his neck. "Don't know. I'd have to talk with Brad about it. I'm sure he would want to do something. Betty worked at the fishery for most of her life."

Jake leaned toward Sean. "Yeah, I can hardly believe she's dead. Murdered."

Sean's eyes widened. "Betty? Why?"

"You haven't heard—a robbery gone bad."

"I tried to stay away from the rumor mill. Betty doesn't have that much."

"That's what Linda said. She and Rachel are at her house, trying to figure out what was stolen. I have a few errands, and then I'm going to help them later." Jake stepped up to the counter to buy his coffee.

"I'll let you know what Brad says about a bigger place for the memorial service." Sean made his way toward the exit.

After Jake ordered his drink, he grabbed a basket and found the aisle for cleaning supplies, staying away from the café section where Brad and Celeste sat.

Jake finished his coffee and paid for the items he bought. When he stepped outside, the chill made him think about what had happened to Betty. Anger swelled in his gut. Why did bad things happen to good people? He'd asked the Lord that many times. Maybe life as a police officer in Anchorage wasn't really for him? And yet, he'd only been home one day and a murder occurred in this usually peaceful town.

He walked around the corner of the large store. When he reached his grandfather's SUV, the rear driver's side tire was flat. He stuck the sack of supplies in the back and got out what he needed to replace it with a spare. As he knelt to fix the jack under the car, he glanced at the front tire—flat like the back one. Jake examined it and found a large slit in it.

This wasn't an accident. Someone did this on purpose.

Carrying a sack of supplies, Rachel stepped into Betty's house, drew in a fortifying breath and said, "Remember this place was trashed."

"I've seen trashed before. Your dad was the messiest guy." Hands full with a mop, broom and garbage bags, Aunt Linda entered a few paces behind Rachel. She glanced at the living room and blew out a rush of air. "Okay. This tops anything your dad did."

"Probably more than one person did this. Going through everything takes time. Jake was stopping by the police station to talk to Chief Quay."

Aunt Linda shook her head as her gaze skimmed over the piles of items on the floor. "I hope Betty didn't see this. Everything in her house had a place, and she kept it that way. Very organized. It will take days to go through, but I'm determined to see if anything is missing. I have a good idea what she has of value that a burglar might want."

"I can't see this as a robbery gone bad. Everyone knows her in town. They know she has limited funds and just makes it every month."

"Where do we start?" Aunt Linda leaned the mop and broom against the wall.

"In here. If we can get this room and her bedroom done today, I'll consider it good, then after church tomorrow, we can come work on the kitchen. It's the worst."

"Sounds like a plan."

"But first, we should check to see if her valuables are still in the hidey-hole in the kitchen."

"Yes, I'm sure the police chief would like to know if anything was taken as soon as possible. It might help him find who did this." Aunt Linda crossed the living room to the kitchen entrance and halted. "This looks like a tornado went through here. Why were they emptying food boxes? What in the world were they looking for?"

"Some people have hidden cash in cereal, flour, whatever."

Aunt Linda harrumphed. "That gives me the willies. What about the germs?"

"Usually they have them in something plastic." Over her aunt's shoulder, Rachel gestured to the open freezer, a puddle of water on the floor nearby. "People have been known to hide money and stuff like that in the freezer."

"Obviously, it didn't work. They checked it. But really, the intruders couldn't have known Betty very well, or they wouldn't have wasted their time."

Rachel thought back to the panicked look on Aunt Betty's face the day before. She could still hear the scared desperation in Aunt Betty's voice in the break room. Why didn't she talk to the local police?

Aunt Linda stepped over the worst of the mess on the floor and covered the distance to the counter area she'd described last night. With her foot, she brushed some empty boxes and cans away, then knelt. She reached into the cubbyhole at the junction of the cabinets. "Got something."

Rachel stooped down behind her aunt. "Do we have anything like this at our house?"

"Nope." Aunt Linda slid out a plastic bag with a few pieces of jewelry and another with several keys and gave them to Rachel, then she stuck her hand back inside. "There's something else. Feels like one of her photos—actually several."

When her aunt drew them out and examined them, Rachel looked over Aunt Linda's shoulder. "That's the shipping room at the fishery. Why would she take a picture of that? She didn't work in that department."

"I don't know. Maybe there are more in her darkroom." Linda glanced back at Rachel. "The camera she used was old—one she had for years. She still used film. That was probably her one luxury. Buying film and what she needed to process her own photos."

"Three pictures are all that's in the cubbyhole?"

"Let me check to make sure. It goes back to the wall." Her aunt rechecked and came up empty-handed. "Before we start cleaning, let's see what's left of her darkroom. Most of her photos are of nature. She is… I mean, she was good. Photography made her happy."

Rachel clasped her shoulder, hearing the pain in her aunt's voice. She leaned over and hugged her. "She's with God now."

Aunt Linda cleared her throat. "I know. But…" She gave her head one hard shake, then pulled herself to her feet. "This isn't getting her house cleaned. Betty would have hated her house this way."

As they made their way to the second bedroom closet, Rachel slipped the items from the hidey-hole into her pocket.

"I remember it took Betty a year to save up for her camera. She was so excited when she finally got it. I bought her enough film that I think it lasted six months, even though she went out every weekend and took pictures of things that interested her."

Rachel dragged the door open, so that Aunt Linda and she could peer into the darkroom side by side in the entrance.

"I don't see her camera," her aunt mumbled, then crouched down and began moving the clutter to see what was under it. "She keeps it in here on the hook by the door. It's not there, and whatever she was processing was destroyed. Could that be the reason someone came to her house?"

The scent of the chemicals still lingered in the air, but something else invaded and began to overpower that odor. Rachel swiveled around and went to the entrance into the bedroom. As she took in a deep breath away from the closet, a whiff of smoke grew stronger.

Rachel hurried into the living room, her gaze riveting to flames licking up the drapes on the front and side of the house.

# FOUR

Jake paced the reception area of Max's Garage while Max changed his second slashed tire and replaced it with a new one. He'd tried calling Rachel at Linda's and then at Betty's house but got no answer. He'd even called his grandfather to send him over to Betty's, but he must still be outside plowing some of the roads for people near them. Why would anyone slash his tires unless they wanted him delayed in town?

The hairs on his nape stood up. Something was wrong, and the only thing he could think about was Rachel and Linda over at Betty's. What if the intruders hadn't found what they were looking for and came back?

He snatched up the receiver to call the police. When the dispatcher answered, he asked, "Is Chief Quay in?"

"No, he's out on a call. In fact, everyone is busy. May I help you?"

"This is Jake Nichols. I was in there earlier. Ask him to go to Betty Marshal's house as soon as possible." Maybe he was overreacting. He hoped he was.

"That was so sad about her being killed yesterday. Is something wrong at her house?"

"Rachel Hart and Linda Thomas were going to Betty's house to clean it up and see if they could discover if anything had been stolen. My tires were slashed when I was parked at the general store, and now no one is answering at Betty's house. I think something could be wrong." Jake looked toward the counter and saw Max with his keys. Jake rose. "I'll be heading there now."

"I'll call the chief and let him know. In the meantime, Officer Bates is nearer. I'll see if he can drive by."

"Thanks." Jake hung up and headed toward Max. "I appreciate the rush."

"I put the new spare in the back. Someone wasn't happy with you. Do you think it's somehow connected to what happened at Betty's?"

Jake shrugged and grabbed his keys. "I don't know, but I don't want to take the chance." Then he started for the car in the bay area in the back.

He pushed his SUV as much as he could

without ending up in a ditch. The unsettled feeling in his gut wouldn't go away. In fact, it grew stronger the closer he got to Betty's house.

His heartbeat kicked up several notches when he spied a plume of smoke billowing in the cloudy sky in the direction where he was heading. He pressed down the accelerator.

"Aunt Linda," Rachel screamed over the crackling of the fire as she raced back to the second bedroom. "We've got to get out of here."

Her aunt rushed out of the darkroom, her eyes round like the full moon a few nights ago. "Why?"

"The living room is on fire."

Aunt Linda hurried past Rachel, and when she reached the end of the hallway, smoke invaded the corridor. Putting her hand over her mouth, her aunt stopped and peered into the living room, a thick gray cloud filling the whole area.

"We can't get out the front door," Rachel said as the fire consumed that part of the house. She swiveled her attention toward the kitchen and noticed smoke mushrooming through the door-way. Grabbing her aunt's arm, she tugged her away. “We can’t get out that way, either. We’ll climb out a window.” But when she hastened into the first bedroom, her gaze fixed on the high windows that allowed sunlight inside but would be hard to climb out of.

“There’s a bigger one in the bathroom. The other bedroom is just like this—a set of high, narrow windows.” Aunt Linda pivoted and raced to the bathroom.

When Rachel rushed inside behind her, she nearly ran into her aunt, who stood still in front of the frosted pane. “It’s smaller than I thought, and the glass is thicker than normal.”

Aunt Linda whirled around, looking for anything to break the window. Nothing. Rachel hurried back to Betty’s bedroom to find something while her aunt checked the second one. In the midst of the clutter on the floor, Rachel didn’t see anything that would break the glass.

Smoke snaked into the room. Rachel pulled her turtleneck over her mouth and continued her search. Her gaze fell on a metal flashlight that might work. She had to try it. She snatched it up and raced back to the bathroom. After putting the toilet seat down, she climbed on top of it and swung the flashlight toward the thick, frosted glass. It bounced off, not even cracking the window.

* * *

Jake pulled into the long driveway to Betty's house, spying Rachel's Jeep. Flames mixed with blackened smoke shot up from the roof of the cabin. He pulled out his cell phone and prayed he had reception. A dead zone. His throat tightened with the thought of what Rachel and Linda must be going through—if they were even still alive. The idea of not seeing Rachel again stole his breath.

*That's not going to happen if I can help it.*

He slammed his SUV into park and jumped from it. The front door blazed as fire ate at the wood around it. He raced to the side of the house, then the back entrance. The same sight greeted him as though someone started the fire at the points of entry. He hurried to the left where the bedrooms were. When his gaze latched on to the long, slender windows at the top of the bedroom, the thundering of his heartbeat vied with the roar of the fire. Then he remembered the other bedroom was the same.

He moved toward the bathroom, trying to imagine what the window was like. Frosted and thick, but he could see movement behind the pane. Someone was still alive. It would be hard, but he thought both Rachel and Linda could fit through the opening.

He swept around, trying to find something to break the glass with. He ran to the shed and found a sledgehammer in the tool closet. When he hurried back to the house, he stood near and shouted, "Get back. I'm going to break the glass."

He lifted the sledgehammer onto his shoulder, praying that whoever was in the bathroom had moved back, but he had no choice. Getting cut was better than dying in a fire. He swung the tool toward the window with all the strength he could muster.

Rachel had tried several more times with the flashlight, then discarded it. Needing something else she climbed down from the toilet. Fingers of smoke crept into the room.

Coughing, her aunt scurried into the bathroom with a shotgun and gave it to Rachel. Then Aunt Linda closed the door and stuffed some towels under it. "We don't have much time. Maybe we could use the gun like a bat or shoot at the glass."

Rachel checked to see if the weapon was loaded. "If shooting doesn't work, we can try the other way." She lifted the shotgun and aimed. Her ears pounded with the beating of her heart. With the noise of the crackling fire coming down the hallway, she put her finger on the trigger.

"Wait. Listen." Aunt Linda grabbed Rachel's arm. "That sounds like Jake."

Something slammed into the window. Her aunt shoved her into the bathtub as the glass exploded into the room. The backs of her legs hit the edge of the tub, and Rachel tumbled backward, her aunt following her. A few shards pierced Rachel's arm as she put it up to block her face. Her body crashed against the hard white acrylic, knocking the breath from her.

"Rachel. Linda," Jake shouted as he appeared in the smashed window.

Aunt Linda rolled off Rachel and replied, "We're okay."

With a sledgehammer, Jake began knocking the rest of the glass out of the frame. "Grab some towels to lay on the ledge. You need to hurry. The fire is working its way to this side."

Her aunt scrambled from the bathtub and held her hand out for Rachel to take. Still trying to catch a decent breath, she gripped her aunt's hand and let her haul her to her feet. Aunt Linda helped her out of the tub and removed the towels from under the door. Smoke poured into the room from every crack around the door seal. It tickled Rachel's throat, and she coughed. She pulled her turtleneck over her month again, but the smoke stung her watering eyes.

"Ready?" Jake took the towels that Aunt Linda gave him and placed them on the ledge. "I'll help you from this side."

"You go first." Rachel helped her aunt up onto the closed toilet seat. She couldn't lose her other aunt. Please, Lord.

The cuts on Rachel's arms hurt, and blood dripped onto the tile floor. She took a washcloth to help stem the flow while Aunt Linda leaned into the window. Rachel helped her out the hole. Her aunt was petite, and she barely made it.

A loud boom shook the house. Rachel glanced back at the door.

"Hurry, Rachel. The fire is spreading over the roof." Urgency filled Jake's voice.

The sound of his voice calmed the fear rising in her even as she climbed onto her perch, leaped to the window and grabbed Jake's hands to hold tight. Her legs dangled in midair in the bathroom. She wriggled her body, trying to move forward, while Jake pulled her toward him. Her side rubbed against the frame, and something sharp scraped her.

She groaned.

"Okay?"

"There must be some glass on my right, but don't stop."

"Sorry, I thought I got all the glass out of the frame."

"Pull harder. My shoulders are barely through, but my hips are bigger."

"Scoot as much to the left as you can. I'll find something to put between you and the frame on the right."

Another crash sounded behind her. Time was running out.

Rachel managed to shift a tad bit while Jake said, "I'll be right back. I remember a piece of flashing in the shed." Jake raced toward the small building.

Without Jake to block the wind, it bombarded Rachel with cold and the scent of smoke and burning wood. Coughs racked her while Jake rushed back. He took the flashing and put it between her and the window frame.

"This should help you move easier." Then he grabbed her arms and yanked.

"Just get me out." She imagined the flames eating away at the door, any second bursting into the room.

He pulled slowly at first, and then the second her hips cleared, she slipped out easily, almost toppling into him.

After moving away from the house, he gathered her into his embrace and held her for a few seconds. "I thought I'd lost you when I saw the house on fire."

She nestled against him, relishing the warmth of him and the sense of safety she felt. In that moment she never wanted to leave the shelter of his arms.

"Are you okay?" he murmured against the top of her head.

She nodded against his chest, then turned within his arms and looked at the cabin nearly consumed totally by the flames. "This was no accident. The fire was at the back and front exits. Even the windows we could have easily been able to escape through were consumed with flames."

Her face ashen and wearing Jake's coat, Aunt Linda stepped closer. "Someone wanted to destroy Betty's house. Why?"

"Good question and one I intend to find out. No one goes after you two without answering to me." Jake's arms cuddled Rachel even closer. "I don't want to go through that again."

"Neither do I," Rachel whispered, her throat raw.

"I'm taking you to town to report this to the police and see the doctor."

Not wanting to leave his arms, Rachel glanced over her shoulder. "Take us home. We'll call the police and report the fire."

"Nope. You need to have Doc look at your injuries." He released her and examined her right side. "You're bleeding. Let's get to Gramps's car. He has some towels you can place over the wound." Jake looked at her aunt. "Are you okay? I didn't see bleeding."

She nodded.

As flames engulfed the cabin, they hurried to the SUV, the sound of sirens filling the air.

A police car came down the long drive followed by the fire department. There wasn't anything that could be done for the cabin. With only a light breeze and a snow-covered ground, hopefully the blaze wouldn't spread.

"See? Now we don't have to go to town." Rachel took the clean towel from Jake and pressed it into her side.

"You're still going to see Doc." Jake started the car and turned the heater on, then he climbed from the vehicle.

"Wait," Aunt Linda said. "Take this." She shed his coat and tossed it toward him.

He caught it and walked toward Chief Quay as he got out of his cruiser.

Rachel watched the conversation between

them with Jake gesturing toward the house, anger creasing his forehead as he spoke to the chief.

"Jake saved us," her aunt murmured.

"I know." Since he'd come home, she felt as though she'd been on a tilt-a-whirl, spinning out of control. And yet, seeing him again renewed feelings she'd kept buried—conflicting emotions from anger at him leaving to happiness he was here.

As Jake returned to the SUV, the firefighters hooked up their equipment. "Let's go. Randall will come out to see you later after you've seen Doc."

"How did he find out about the fire since we couldn't call it in?"

"Gramps saw the black smoke when he returned from plowing the Andersons' drive down the road. He went home, placed the call and then was going to come over. Randall told him that he just received a report from another neighbor and he would take care of it." Jake backed up, then made a turn and headed for the highway.

Jake opened Linda's door to greet his grandfather and Mitch. "Thanks for bringing him over. Randall should be here soon to interview Rachel and Linda."

"The cabin must have gone up quickly." Gramps entered while Jake petted Mitch.

"Probably an accelerant was used. One of the firefighters has experience in determining arson."

"That makes sense." Gramps sat on the couch. "Where are Linda and Rachel?"

"Changing. Doc had to sew up Rachel's right side where some glass sliced her good. The rest of her cuts were small. Neither of them have smoke inhalation problems." As Jake rattled off the list of injuries, a part of him was back at the cabin, frantically trying to get Rachel free. If something had happened to her, he would have blamed himself. He'd rescued many people while working for the Northern Frontier Search and Rescue Organization and the police, so he should be able to save someone he really cared about.

"That's a relief. I should have gone with them this morning."

"And what? From what they told me it happened fast, and there wasn't anything that could be done, except to get out. Besides, you wouldn't have fit through the window."

"True. I never thought something like that would happen."

"Neither did I or I would have been there."

Gramps's wrinkled face cracked a big grin. "Do I need to say if you had, you wouldn't have gotten out? We have the same build. Most of the Nichols men are tall and have broad shoulders."

Jake chuckled. "Touché."

"It's good to hear some laughter after the day I've had," Rachel said as she walked slowly into the living room.

Jake turned toward her, remembering how close he'd come to losing her. That thought left his gut roiling, and he was even more determined to find out what was going on in Port Aurora. "Are you all right?" He took in her pale face and tired eyes—a beautiful sight to see. It could have gone so wrong today.

"My side hurts, but it felt great to take a shower and get that smoke smell out of my hair. I think I washed it three times."

When Rachel moved past him to the chair across from Gramps, Jake drew in a deep breath of the apple-scented shampoo. She still used the same one from when she was a child. He associated apples with Rachel because of that.

She eased down, wincing once. "When is the chief arriving?"

"I see his car coming down the road." Linda crossed the room and opened the door to the arctic entry.

After shaking Randall's hand, Jake sat next to Rachel's aunt on the couch while the chief took the last chair. His grim expression fit Jake's mood. Every alarm bell was going off in his head. The fire only reinforced his belief that Betty's death wasn't due to a robbery gone bad. What had Betty gotten herself into?

"Are you two all right now?" the chief asked, withdrawing a pad and pen from his pocket.

"As well as could be expected." Linda pressed her lips together.

Randall shifted his attention to Rachel. "I understand Doc had to see you."

"I'll be okay. Do you have any idea what happened?"

"No, other than there were footprints leading to the house from the woods on the left side. I followed them to tire tracks—probably a truck. I'm treating this fire as arson at this time. Did either of you see anything?"

Linda shook her head while Rachel said, "We were in the back bedroom, looking for Aunt Betty's camera."

"Why?"

"Although I don't think it is worth much except to her, someone could have taken it," Linda answered Randall.

"Did you find it?"

"No, but I didn't check the darkroom thoroughly. It was trashed like the whole place was. The camera usually hangs on the peg by the door, but it wasn't there."

The chief wrote on his pad. "So it's possible that a camera was stolen. Anything else you know of?"

"We found her few pieces of jewelry that were worth something, although not that much." Rachel withdrew the ring and two sets of earrings still in the plastic bag. "And as you know, the television and small appliances like the food processor were still in the house, so truthfully I don't think anything else was missing, but we'll never know for sure."

"I wonder if the camera might be the reason the cabin was torched." Randall wrote something else on the paper, then glanced at Linda, then Rachel.

"It was a ten-year-old Kodak that was special to Betty, but I couldn't see it bringing much money for anyone who stole it. It wasn't even digital." Linda combed her fingers through her wet, short blond hair.

"Anything else?" Randall asked.

Her gaze trained on Rachel, Linda furrowed her brow but remained quiet. Rachel shook her head slightly. Was there more that Rachel wasn't saying? Randall didn't seem to pick up the exchanged looks between them, but when he left, Jake would be asking them about it.

"If I think of anything, I'll call you," Rachel finally said. "Please let us know the progress on the case. Aunt Betty never had any enemies in town. She was always one of the first to help others."

Randall stood and pocketed his pad and pen. "It's most disturbing to me. She is the last person I would expect to be murdered."

"So you're ruling her death a murder for sure?" Jake rose to escort the police chief to the door.

"Yes, we are. And we're taking the investigation very seriously."

Jake opened the door for Randall. "I'd like to check the cabin site after it cools. Is that okay?"

"Sure, after the firefighters give the go-ahead." Randall tipped his head toward the ladies. "I'm glad you're both okay. Good day."

At the window Jake watched Randall climb into his car before he swung around and asked, “What are you two keeping from the police chief?”

# FIVE

Rachel sat forward. "How did you know?"

"I may have been gone for a while, but I know when you're holding something back."

Rachel stared at her aunt. "We don't know who to trust. We don't believe Aunt Betty's murder was done by a person passing through town. It's not like Port Aurora is on the beaten path. If this had been summer, it might be different."

Lawrence narrowed his gaze on Aunt Linda. "You think we have something to do with Betty's murder?"

"Of course not. That's why Rachel is telling you two. We also found three photos of the fishery in Betty's special cubbyhole. That was why I was looking in the darkroom, but there was no sign of other pictures being processed or the camera. If more photos were being developed, they were either ruined when the intruders trashed the house or taken by them."

Rachel sat on the edge of her chair. "Why would she keep in her hidey-hole three pictures, one of the Tundra King and the Alaskan King next to each other, the Blue Runner and the shipping warehouse?"

"Where are they?" Jake asked in a no-nonsense tone.

"On my dresser." Rachel pushed to her feet. "I'll get them. Maybe you can explain why these were special to her that she hid them with her valuables."

"In the meantime, I'm starving. I'm going to make some sandwiches. Anyone else want one?" Aunt Linda strolled toward the kitchen.

"I do, and I'll help you." Lawrence followed her aunt while Jake accepted the offer of food.

"Me, too, Aunt Linda. Escaping a fire wore me out." Rachel retrieved the photos and returned to the living room to find Jake standing next to the decorated Christmas tree, staring out the window. She came up beside him. "It's starting to get dark. No wonder I'm hungry. I haven't eaten since seven this morning." She held out the pictures.

Jake took them and studied each one. "I'm

familiar with the Tundra King. Is the Alaskan King a new boat to Port Aurora?"

"Yes, it's a new addition from Seattle. When Brad acquired a silent partner, he purchased a couple of trawlers that belonged to the fishery as well as overhauling the Tundra King. That brings his fleet up to ten boats. The rest are independently owned but sell their catches to us."

"Who captains the Blue Runner?"

"Still Tom Payne. He was sweet on Aunt Betty. She thought of him as a friend. After her abusive husband died, she didn't want to get serious with anyone else. Tom understood that. But that reminds me, I need to talk to him. Maybe Aunt Betty said something to him about what she wanted to talk to me about. His boat is due back Monday. He and his crew went out crabbing on Wednesday."

"So they were good friends?"

"Yes." Rachel took the picture of both the Tundra King and Alaskan King and the Blue Runner and studied them. "That might be when Aunt Betty took this photo. It looks like the Tundra King just arrived at the pier while the Blue Runner is getting ready to leave. That coincides with the date on the back of the pictures. It's daylight and Aunt Betty might have taken them on her lunch hour."

"If she was worried about something, why didn't she say anything to Linda? Or you at that time? You all are family."

"I don't know. Maybe it was something she didn't think Aunt Linda should know, or she was going to tell her sister and me when we finally talked. We may never know."

"Hey, you two. Are you hungry? Dinner—or whatever you want to call a meal at three in the afternoon—is ready in the kitchen."

After they were all seated and Lawrence blessed the food, silence fell over them for five minutes while they satisfied their hunger.

Eventually, Rachel broke the quiet. "Do you think I should give the police chief these photos? They really don't show anything but three boats and the shipping warehouse, and I think Tom would love to have the one of the Blue Runner."

Jake's intense regard took her in for a long moment while her aunt and Lawrence discussed what the photos meant. Finally, Jake said, "I think you should give them to Randall. I know the man, and he was a good pick to run the department. I worked under him, and I never had a reason to question his integrity."

"So you think I should tell him that Aunt Betty wanted to talk to you and me?" Rachel asked, still trapped by his penetrating gaze as though no one else was in the kitchen but them. Her heartbeat accelerated, and she wiped her sweaty palms on her pants.

"Yes. He can't do his job if he doesn't have all the pieces." Jake glanced at the photos in the center of the table, releasing her from the invisible tether connecting them.

Her stomach tightened. What was going on with her? Granted, she hadn't seen Jake in a few years, but she shouldn't be reacting to him like this. Their lives were on different paths.

"I'm not sure they have any significance to Betty's murder, but he needs to rule them out. The first one is of the Tundra King and Alaskan King unloading their catch at the loading dock. The second is Blue Runner in its slip. The third is boxes stacked in a room, which you said looked like part of the new shipping warehouse." Jake picked it up and flipped it over to show the date. "Since these may have been the last photos Betty took, maybe they will help Randall."

"Son, we haven't talked about someone slashing your tires earlier. If they hadn't, you'd have seen the fire much earlier or even come upon the persons who set it." Gramps took another bite of his turkey and Swiss sandwich.

Jake frowned. "To tell you the truth, with all that has happened, I haven't had time to think about it, but you're right. I only went to the police to find out what progress had been made on the case, then to the general store for the supplies. I came out and my tires were slashed."

"Did you say anything about what happened at Betty's cabin to anyone?" Rachel finished the last of her sandwich and relaxed back, trying to ease the tension gripping her, not just from nearly dying in the fire but from Jake, too.

"I mentioned it to Randall at the police station and told Sean that you and Linda were at the house cleaning it up. Anyone in earshot could have overheard that I was getting supplies and going to Betty's cabin to help you. When I couldn't get hold of you two at Betty's or your house, I left Max's Garage and headed that way."

Lawrence slapped his hand on the table. "That's it. Someone heard and didn't want you to go. You need to make a list of who was at the store and station besides Randall."

"Well, except for Randall, Officers Bates

and Clark were at the station. It was just the people at the store and frankly, I can't remember all of them. There were some who I couldn't even tell you their names. Marge was behind the counter, and I saw Celeste and Brad."

*He saw Celeste? Why didn't he say something to me?* Rachel balled her hands in her lap. *How did he feel? Is he still in love with her? I hate being shut out of that part of his life.*

"Linda, I was going to stop at the church on the way back to Betty's, but forgot all about that after my tires were slashed." He looked toward her aunt. "Sorry about that. But I did talk to Sean in the store about using a larger venue at the fishery for the memorial service. He reminded me how many people Betty had known and would want to pay their respects. The church won't be able to hold all of them."

Aunt Linda began taking the empty dishes to the sink. "Thanks for letting me know about the church. I'll call our pastor this evening and get his take on where to hold the memorial service. Betty wanted to be cremated. We can sprinkle her remains in Bristol Bay. I think Tom would let us use the Blue Runner. In fact, I'm sure he would insist."

"What did Celeste have to say?" Rachel

finally asked, not wanting to talk about her but wanting to know how it went with Jake. At one time she and Celeste had been friends, but after Jake, that had all changed.

"Nothing. She and Brad were eating. I'm not even sure they saw me."

Lawrence rose and headed for the sink. "I'll help you clean up, then you might offer me some of that pie left over from last night."

"Anyone else want a piece?" Aunt Linda asked as she handed Lawrence a dish to dry.

Rachel groaned. "I think I'll pass."

Her aunt gave her a puzzled look. "But it's your favorite. I was counting on your helping me finish it today."

"I need to go on a diet after today, trying to squeeze out of that window."

"I'll take an extra big piece," Jake said.

Rachel leaned closer to him and whispered, "Are you okay with seeing Celeste?"

He lifted one shoulder in a shrug. "I knew I would see her eventually. She doesn't mean anything to me."

Rachel wasn't convinced by his casual tone. He'd walked away from Port Aurora, his grandfather—her—all because of Celeste. "I'm here if you need to talk to anyone about her."

"She's my past. Let's leave her there."

*But are you over your past?* Rachel gritted her teeth to keep from replying. An uncomfortable silence fell between her and Jake. She took the last sip of her cold coffee and stood. "Do you want a refill?"

"Yes, thanks."

She grabbed Jake's mug and headed for the stove when her aunt stepped back from the sink, put her hands on her hips and said to Lawrence, "Jake is going to do what?" Her voice rose.

Rachel's gaze flew to Jake.

He stood. "Gramps, what did you say to her?"

"I told her what you and I talked about. Somebody's got to protect these gals. What if the people who burned Betty's house come after them? Remember that conversation we had a couple of hours ago?"

Jake glanced between Aunt Linda and her. "I was going to bring it up and see what you thought." He swiveled his attention back to his grandfather. "Nothing was settled between Gramps and me."

Lawrence waved his hand in the air. "They are both sensible, practical women. They will see it's for their own good."

Aunt Linda's eyes flared. "Our own good?"

She tossed the wet dishcloth at Lawrence's chest. "I answer to no man. I've done just fine for fifteen years since my husband died."

Rachel grabbed hold of Jake's hand and dragged him from the kitchen as her aunt became worked up. "What are you and your grandfather scheming?"

"It's possible that whoever killed Betty thinks you know something about her murder. If you're in danger, we need to protect you."

"But I don't know anything."

"You might not realize what you know. Something is going on in Port Aurora. I don't know what, but two people went to a lot of trouble to shut up Betty. I'd feel better if you let me stay here with Mitch. He's a great watchdog on top of everything else."

"What if you're in danger? Your tires were slashed today. People know how close we once were. They might think you also know whatever it is that I'm supposed to know."

"I was trained to take care of myself. I'd like to take you to and from work. You're too important to me to have anything happen to you. And in case you haven't noticed, my grandfather is as he says *sweet on* Linda."

"But she only thinks of him as a friend."

Jake stepped into her personal space and

grasped her upper arms. "Do you know what would happen if you and your aunt were hurt? Gramps and I would be devastated. Being a friend to you means a lot to me. Gramps feels the same way about Linda."

Over the loud conversation coming from the kitchen, Rachel asked what she'd wanted to for years. "Then why did you leave and not come back until now?"

"I needed to get out of the city. As soon as I was released from physical therapy, I came home, and I'm staying until the new year."

"Eight years is a long time to be apart."

"I saw you several times, and we talked on the phone."

"Not the same thing. Remember when we were teenagers and something would go wrong with one of us at school? We would talk about it all the way home that very day."

Jake released her arms and put some distance between them. "When Celeste called off our engagement, I'd felt like I'd been abandoned. It was my mother all over again. I didn't process it well."

"That's what having a friend means. I could have helped you."

"I couldn't stick around and be constantly

reminded of what she did. See her all the time. This is a small town."

"So you're still in love with her." Acid burned in her stomach, threatening to send her meal back up. She'd always felt when Jake finally made a commitment it would be forever.

"No!" His face hardened into sharp angles. "When I saw them together, I didn't care. I felt nothing."

She wanted to believe that was the case, but he'd stayed away for eight years. That didn't sound like a man who was over Celeste. She didn't want to be dragged back into his life, then have him leave in four weeks.

"Why are we wasting time talking about her? She's married. I don't love her, and she has nothing to do with someone trying to kill you."

"We don't know someone's trying to kill me. Maybe the killers came back today to burn the house because they didn't find everything they wanted, and Aunt Linda and I just happened to be inside at that time."

"Do you want to take the chance with your life and your aunt's?"

He was right. She had no problem with a man protecting her. Her aunt might, but she could talk her into it. And an added bonus would be having a watchdog. "Fine. You can stay and be my chauffeur, starting with tomorrow when I go to church."

"I'll drop you off and—"

"Jake Nichols, you always went to church when you lived here. But then maybe it's best you don't."

His forehead crunched. "Why?"

"Brad and Celeste usually attend every Sunday."

He glared at her. "I know what you're doing."

She batted her eyelashes. "What am I doing?"

"Challenging me. You know how I am. We'll both go to church tomorrow. Then you and I can go see Randall with the photos."

"He might not be working on Sunday."

"Then we'll go to his house. If someone's after those pictures, you giving them to the police ends the threat on your life. In fact, we should go right now."

"But there's nothing suspicious on those photos, and no one knows I have them. After the horrible day I've had, all I want is to go to bed early."

"Maybe there is and we can't see it, or maybe the arsonists thought there was more than what was in the darkroom. You said that

Betty takes tons of pictures to get the right one she wants to use."

"I've convinced Lawrence to stay here tonight, too," her aunt announced from the entrance into the kitchen. "I don't like the idea of him being alone with all that's going on."

Lawrence snorted behind her. "I know how to take care of myself. I have for seventy-three years."

Aunt Linda shot him a glare. "I think we should stick together until the police find who murdered Betty and torched her house."

Jake came up and laid his hands on Rachel's shoulders, then he leaned close to her ear. "I think your aunt has a thing for my grandfather, too." His chuckles slid deliciously down her spine.

Rachel was beginning to wonder if she had *a thing* for Jake.

Monday morning Jake drove into town with Rachel. "You have some time to grab a cup of coffee at the general store? I could use another one before I meet Randall at Betty's house."

"That sounds good. This was one weekend I didn't rest. I'm more exhausted this morning than I was Friday when I left work."

"Nearly dying can do that to a person." He slanted a look at her. "Take it from me."

"I still wish you'd let your grandfather call me in August. Finding out after you were out of danger robbed me of praying for you when you needed it the most."

"I was in a dark place. I thought I'd lost Mitch and might not walk again. I had no words for anyone." Jake pulled into a parking spot in front of the store, remembering the last time he was here and his tires were slashed.

After they purchased their coffees at the counter, Jake found a table, one of the last in the crowded café, and sat with his back to the wall. "If I see anyone I recognize was here on Saturday morning, I'll tell you. I knew the town had grown, but there are a lot of people I don't know. I discovered that yesterday at church."

"I've been here the whole time, and I feel that way sometimes. In the summer the tourist season nearly doubles the town's population, and there are more fishing boats going out then, too."

Jake sipped his coffee. "I'm meeting Sean for lunch at the harbor restaurant. I hope to find out what Betty was like the few days before she was murdered."

"I'm going to see Tom on the Blue Runner. I know he's been told about Aunt Betty over the radio, but that's no way to learn about it. All he knows is she's dead. Since Chief Quay is letting me give him the photo she took of his boat, I thought I would also use the time to make sure he's all right and see if she said anything to him that concerned her."

"What time are you meeting him?"

"He'll unload his catch, then be in his slip around twelve."

"I can't be there, but hearing the details of what happened to Betty is better coming from you than a police officer." He covered her hand on the table. "Remember, leave the detecting to me or Randall. Tell him about Betty but no snooping."

"He's one of the people we know didn't kill Aunt Betty. He was at sea with his crew."

"True, but he could have hired someone."

"Do you always think that way?"

"I look at all the angles. I've seen a lot of stuff that people do to each other, even ones who are supposed to be in love."

Rachel shook her head. "I've seen how Tom was with Aunt Betty. He cherished her."

"I've broken up many couples who supposedly loved each other." After his own experience and some of the people he encountered as a police officer, he didn't know if love between a man and woman really existed. "Can you get me the names of the boats and crews not in harbor? That should help us eliminate them or at least move them to the bottom of the list of suspects."

"Yes. I know some because I deliver their paychecks on Fridays. I'll make a list, then you should get with Charlie, the harbormaster, to make sure I have everyone."

"So Charlie Moore is doing that job now. If anyone knows who was there or not, it would be him."

"He may have a bum leg that keeps him from working on a trawler, but he gets around and keeps an eye on all the boats. You should see him in the summer. He seems to always be around in the daylight, which means he puts in a lot of hours."

"Does he get any rest in the winter?"

"You'd think." Rachel chuckled. "I guess he does, but he still knows what's going on."

"I'll have to stop by and talk to Charlie myself." Jake caught sight of a familiar face. "The big guy coming into the store. Who is he? He was here on Saturday."

Rachel scanned the people coming inside.

"That's Beau Cohen. He works on the Tundra King. They're going out in a few hours. His brother, Kirk, is the captain."

"Ah, a crewman from one of the boats in the photos. Who is he talking to?"

"Ingrid. I'm surprised she isn't at work by now. She works in the processing center. So many of the people new to Port Aurora are connected to the fishery. At least I know their names and most of their faces."

"When do you think the memorial service will be held for Betty?"

"Now that Brad has offered the large hall in the fishery, Aunt Linda told me she and the pastor were planning it for Wednesday late afternoon. Then later is the Christmas tree lighting at the harbor. Aunt Betty always loved that, and Aunt Linda thought that would be a nice way to end the service. Most of the boats will be in harbor, and many of the crew members knew Aunt Betty. She worked at the fishery for years."

"Since when does the fishery have a large hall?"

"It's temporary until the spring when the processing plant will be expanded, which means more workers. That's the last part of the expansion. It should be up and running by

June." Rachel glanced at her watch. "Oh, no. I'm going to be late."

"If I don't see you, when do you want me to pick you up?"

"Five."

"I'll be at your office then."

"I can meet you outside." She rose.

"I'd like to see where you work." Jake started to get up, but Rachel waved him down.

"I only have to go a block. I think I can do that. Enjoy the warmth and the coffee. See you later."

As she left the store, stopping several times to speak to someone, Jake realized he'd missed her. It hadn't taken long for them to get back into the groove of sharing and talking. He had friends in Anchorage, but no one like Rachel. She was special. In all the years he'd known her, she'd always been there for him. What would have happened if he hadn't left Port Aurora eight years ago?

He'd thought being in Anchorage would be the change of pace he needed to get over Celeste. But now he was back because he'd needed the quiet of the town—and if he was honest with himself, Rachel. She'd always had a way of helping him to see things in a clearer light.

He sighed and headed for the counter to get a cup of coffee to go. When he pulled in to Betty's driveway later, he saw the fire captain shake hands with Randall, then walk to his vehicle. From the grim lines on both men's faces, Jake knew the verdict was arson, which didn't surprise him at all. He finished the last few sips of his coffee, then climbed from the SUV and strode toward the burned remains of the cabin, the scent of charred wood filling his nostrils.

"Captain found three places where an accelerant was used to start the fire. By the front door and window, on one side by the kitchen window and by the back door. It's obvious they didn't want anyone getting out." Randall pointed toward the first area.

"Yeah, I agree. The bedroom windows would have been impossible, and the bathroom one was iffy. I think when they searched the place the day before they either found some of what they wanted or nothing and decided to come back the next morning and burn it to destroy whatever was inside. Did the captain okay the site to be examined?"

"Yes. In this weather, it doesn't take long for the ashes to cool. I've walked the perimeter and seen little evidence that anything survived.

I especially looked at the place where Betty's cubbyhole would have been."

Jake walked toward the crime scene. "I agree, but I still would like to see if anything that looked like a camera was in the darkroom area. It might not have been in its usual place on the hook."

"Or the killers took it the day before. I have to meet with the mayor. If you find anything, let me know. So you really think Betty stumbled across something and took pictures of it? I don't see anything on the photos I looked at yesterday."

"Honestly, I don't know what to think, but if it had been a robbery gone bad, why would they come back the next day to burn the cabin? They knew someone was inside because Rachel's Jeep was out front."

"I agree." Randall started for his cruiser. "I appreciate any help you can give me. As I mentioned, we're an officer short and will be through Christmas."

As the police chief drove away, Jake carefully picked his way through the burned rubble to the place where he estimated the darkroom had been. After sifting through the remains in a ten-foot radius, he straightened and stretched to work the kinks out of his muscles from bending and squatting. He found nothing but the overpowering scent of charred wood.

The hairs on the nape of his neck tingled. He rotated in a full circle, searching the woods that edged Betty's property. A movement in the midst of the spruce trees riveted his attention. He started for the woods, glad he had brought his Glock. Suddenly, the sound of an ATV filled the quiet. Knowing he couldn't outrun a vehicle, he stopped and studied the trees. Nothing. Had someone been watching him?

# SIX

"I'll see you at the memorial service on Wednesday." Rachel waved goodbye to Charlie at the harbormaster's office and stepped outside into the bright sunlight.

Although a chilly wind blew off the water, the rays warmed her. She paused at the railing and scanned the various sizes of boats in port. Spying the Blue Runner tying up to its slip, she strolled toward the trawler. She was not looking forward to talking to Tom Payne. She'd gone over what she was going to say, only to discard it. Tom had made no bones that he loved Aunt Betty, whereas she wasn't eager to marry again. Rachel certainly understood not wanting to marry after having an abusive husband. She didn't want to marry after seeing her mother go from one husband to the next, as though she were sampling an array. She'd seen few examples of a loving marriage.

As she neared the Blue Runner slip, she felt eyes boring into her. She looked around, her gaze skipping from one boat to the next. Finally, it lit upon the Tundra King maneuvering out of the harbor. On the deck she caught sight of Beau dressed in the common yellow outerwear that protected fishermen from the bitter cold wind and water. He brought the binoculars he'd been using down to his side, but she still felt the singe of his perusal. She shuddered.

Rachel shook off her apprehension about Beau. He'd once asked her out on a date, and she had turned him down. Ever since then, he'd been standoffish and almost hostile, which only confirmed he wasn't the type of man she wanted to go out with. She rarely dated, even though there were over twice as many men in Port Aurora as women, but if she did, it wouldn't be someone like Beau.

She stepped down onto the Blue Runner and called out, "Captain Payne?"

A tall man with bright red hair poked his head out the back door into the cabin. "Good to see you, Rachel. If you hadn't been here, I was going to find you at your office. Come in. While the men are finishing up, let's talk in the wheelhouse. It'll be quiet there."

When she entered, Tom's stoic expression

evolved into a look of sorrow. "I almost came in early, but that wouldn't be right for the crew. They count on the money they get, and that depends on the catch." He indicated the captain's chair. "Take a seat. I'm too agitated to stay still. What happened to Betty? She was fine on Wednesday when I left."

As Tom paced the length of the wheelhouse and back, Rachel told him about Friday and finding Aunt Betty's body in the woods. "The police are investigating it as a murder. What you might not know is that the next day someone set fire to her cabin. Aunt Linda and I were over at her place trying to straighten it."

"Yeah, Betty..." His voice faded, and he swallowed hard several times. "She would have hated the mess." He stopped at the front window and stared outside. "What I don't understand is why anyone would kill one of the sweetest women in Port Aurora."

"I agree. We don't understand why, either. Earlier that day she'd told me she needed to talk to me. She looked afraid. She'd wanted to talk to Jake, too. I tried to get her to tell me what was wrong when I saw her at the processing center after she left me a message on my phone, but she just said 'later.' I figured she didn't want to talk until we were alone, so that was why I stopped by on the way home from work. Do you have an idea why she would put this photo—" she passed him the one of the Blue Runner "—along with photos of the Tundra King and Alaskan King and a storage area in the shipping warehouse in her hiding place, or why she would be afraid?"

He shook his head, tears welling into his eyes. "I didn't know she had a hiding place. At the house?"

"Yes, in the kitchen, but the cabin was nearly burned to the ground."

"Then how did you get this?"

"The police chief wanted to know what, if anything, was stolen. The TV and other items a robber might steal were still there. But we never found her camera. We checked the cubbyhole for the few pieces of jewelry that are worth something. They were there, along with these photos. We were in the process of examining the darkroom when I smelled smoke and discovered the fire in the living room and kitchen."

"When I left last Wednesday, she was excited. She was starting to work on her photos of the harbor, the boats and the fishery. She'd had pictures of the fishery before the expansion, and she wanted some after."

"So she wasn't upset?"

He plowed his fingers through his red hair, then massaged his nape. "No, the opposite. She said she would have some to show me when I returned." He blinked, and a tear rolled down his tan cheek.

Rachel gestured toward the photo he still held. "Chief Quay said you could keep that. He made a copy of it, but he didn't see how it was tied to her murder."

"I remember when she took it. She'd been on the boat and had left to go back to work. She shared her lunch with me on..." He closed his eyes. "I'm sorry. I need time alone."

Rachel stood and gave Tom a hug. "I understand. If you remember anything that might have upset her on Friday, please let me know."

"I will," he said in a thick voice.

"I can find my own way out."

"Thanks for giving me this photo." His chest rose and fell as he expelled a long breath.

Rachel climbed onto the dock and started back toward the fishery headquarters. She still had a lot of work to do this afternoon before Jake picked her up. She needed to catch up on the paperwork that was put on hold because of last Friday's payroll, especially since she would be taking off half a day on Wednesday to help set up Aunt Betty's memorial service.

When she entered the building, Brad walked into the lobby with his wife, Celeste. Rachel greeted them. She received a cool reception from Celeste, but Brad was always polite and gentlemanly. She wondered if Celeste ever felt bad about how she'd treated Jake. Calling off an engagement in front of half the town wasn't the best way to do it.

"Rachel, wait a sec," Brad said as he opened the front door for Celeste and gave her a quick kiss on the cheek. When his wife left, he turned toward Rachel. "What can I do for the memorial service?"

"You've already done it by letting us use the hall. It will hold twice what the church will."

"Did you talk with Tom yet?"

"Yes, and he didn't take it well."

"I'm not surprised. He proposed to Betty the weekend before last." Only five feet eight inches, Brad always seemed taller by the way he carried himself, but at the moment his shoulders were hunched. "I didn't think Tom would ever marry."

"The same with Aunt Betty. She never said anything about the proposal."

"She told Tom she had to think about it. She

was going to give him her answer when he returned from this last fishing trip." Brad began strolling down the main hall toward his office.

"Oh," was all Rachel could think to say. Why didn't Aunt Betty say anything to her and Aunt Linda? Most unusual. Was that what Aunt Betty wanted to talk to her about on Friday? Then why did she want to talk to Jake, too?

"Tell Linda I can contribute money for the food, whatever she needs."

"I will. Thanks." Rachel rounded the corner and hurried toward her office at the back of the building.

Once there, she started working her way through the pile of papers on her desk while she ate her sandwich. The hours flew by and before she knew it, Jake stood in her doorway, watching her, with Mitch on a leash next to him.

"It's five already?" She glanced behind her at the dark landscape out the window.

"Afraid so. I can wait a while in the lobby if you want." Jake moved to her desk. "I brought Mitch. He wanted to get out of the house."

"Oh, he told you that?"

"Yes, he did. He brought me his leash."

Rachel laughed. "I like a dog that knows his

own mind." She reached toward the German shepherd and began to rub his head.

Mitch stepped back and sniffed her hand, then sat and barked twice.

Not sure what just happened, Rachel glanced toward Jake. His frown unnerved her. "What's wrong with him?"

"That's his signal when he smells illegal drugs."

"On me?" Rachel stared at the hand Mitch smelled. "I haven't been handling any drugs. Just papers all afternoon."

"What kind of papers?"

"Lists from each boat of the crewmen and hours they worked. Also shipping notices and orders. The typical paperwork that needs to be put in the books."

"Where are they?"

Rachel waved to a foot-tall stack on the table behind her.

"Step out in the hall and let me see what has triggered his response."

Rachel moved to the corridor and leaned against the wall while Jake released Mitch by the entrance and commanded him to find the drugs. Starting on his right, the German shepherd sniffed around the room until he came to the pile of paper she'd been recording. He sat and barked again.

When Rachel came back into her office, she asked, "Could this be what Aunt Betty found out?"

"Possibly. Can you take this stack home with you without being detected? Then I can spread them out and see which sheets have the strongest scent on them."

"Yes, but I shuffled them into different piles before putting them in that stack. If it could transfer to my hands, then why not to other pieces of paper?"

"It could. But maybe I can narrow it down some. If I take Mitch through all the boats and the fishery, we could scare off whoever is handling drugs. It could be something as simple as a worker dealing or taking drugs or a bigger problem than that."

Rachel grabbed a canvas bag and stuffed the papers into it. "Bigger problem?"

"That the fishery is being used by someone to smuggle drugs."

"I've worked with most of these people for years. Your grandfather worked for the company up until five years ago. I…" What happened to Aunt Betty made more sense if large amounts of money were involved.

"As a police officer I've seen a lot of illegal drugs on the streets. It's a big business."

Rachel stared down at her hands. "I hope I can get this smell off me." She wondered how many times in the past she'd handled something that had the same scent. She grabbed her coat and purse. "Let's go."

"We can't tell anyone about this except Linda and Gramps."

"Not the police?"

A hard edge entered his blue eyes, darkened to a stormy sea color. "No, not even the chief, at least for the time being. If I could keep this from Linda and Gramps, I would, but I don't see how we can since they are already involved with Betty's murder. Not much gets past my grandfather."

"Nor my aunt. She'll probably be wondering why I'm scrubbing my hands over and over."

"Not much gets past a dog. One trained to smell blood can find where a drop of blood has been cleaned up."

"That's amazing."

"K-9s are being used more and more for various jobs. Their sense of smell is much keener than ours." Jake held the door open for Rachel.

When she stepped outside into the dark of night, the lights from the harbor and the fishery taunted her. How pervasive was this problem in Port Aurora? Now murder and drugs? What was happening in her small, peaceful hometown?

That night Jake stood outside while Mitch sniffed around. The air was crisp and cold, but clear, too. The silence surrounding Jake helped him to relax after a day spent running down leads that hadn't gone anywhere. He'd searched the woods by Betty's cabin and sure enough there were ATV tracks coming from the main road and going back that way. Someone had been in the trees watching. A curious person or one involved with what happened to Betty?

He heard the door open and glanced back. Rachel came outside, carrying two mugs. The colored lights from the Christmas tree and on the house reflected on the snow and bathed her in their glow.

She gave him a cup. "Hot chocolate with one big marshmallow."

"You remembered?"

"Of course. In the cold months that was our drink." They used to do almost everything together—until Celeste came along and he thought he could have it all. The woman. Marriage. The career he wanted. Why hadn't he seen through Celeste's charade? Now he didn't know what he wanted.

Rachel took a sip of her drink, ending up with marshmallow on her upper lip. "Do I have a mustache?"

"Yes, and that hasn't changed, either."

"It's because I like three marshmallows in my hot chocolate." She licked her tongue over the area. "Did I get it all?"

"Yes, but you might as well wait until you're finished with your drink."

"Good advice as always." She released a long sigh and stared up at the sky. "It's gorgeous. Not a cloud around and a million stars."

"I forget how clear the view is away from the city."

"I should have turned off the Christmas lights. It would have been perfect."

"Nah. I like them. They're welcoming."

She angled toward him. "I thought you were going to tell Aunt Linda and Lawrence about the drugs."

"Since they both were exhausted with planning the memorial service and went to bed, I think we can get away with them not knowing anything until we know more."

"That sounds fine. How long is Mitch going to take?"

"He finished five minutes ago. I just like the quiet."

"And I came out and ruined it."

"No, you came out and joined me. We're sharing the stars." That thought eased the tension thinking about Celeste had caused. In the years he'd been gone, he'd been sure he had dealt with the betrayal and the bitterness his relationship with Celeste had produced. Was Rachel right? Was he not over her? No, when he saw Celeste, he'd felt nothing.

He slung his arm over Rachel's shoulder and looked again at the black sky overhead. Their closeness brought back fond memories, something he'd needed after the past months. Peace wove its way through him, and he didn't want this moment to end. Rachel snuggled closer, sending his pulse zipping through him.

"I've missed this," he murmured, not realizing how much until he said it out loud. Rachel had always been the bright spot in his life. Every birthday and Christmas when he wouldn't receive a call or present from his mother, Rachel had cheered him up and given him her gift.

Suddenly, Mitch became alert, emitting a low growl.

Jake dropped his arm from around Rachel

and straightened, handing her his mug. "Stay here." All his police training coming to the foreground, he moved toward Mitch, twenty feet away.

He approached Mitch. "Stay."

His dog did, but he pointed at attention at an area on the west side of the house. Jake wished he had his weapon, but it was in the house.

Then he noticed the huge moose in the moonlight, and relief replaced the stress. Although he had a healthy respect for the damage a moose could cause, he wasn't worried about this one. He was sure the animal knew they were there, and yet he ignored them.

He started back toward Rachel. "Come, Mitch. Time to go in."

"What was it?" she asked in a shaky voice.

"A moose."

"Oh, that's Fred. He comes around once or twice a week. Sometimes during the day. Sometimes at night."

"How do you know it was Fred?"

"Was he missing part of his antler?"

"Yes."

"Then it's him. He's been around for years. He started coming not long after you left Port Aurora."

"Good to know." Jake held the door open

and let Rachel and Mitch go inside, then he gave one last look across the snow-covered ground to the line of evergreens about thirty yards away. Darkness loomed in the depth of the forest.

"I'll get the canvas bag. Let's get this over with." Rachel headed for her bedroom and returned in half a minute. "I think I should handle the papers. You don't need to get the smell on you."

"Fine." Jake sat on the couch where he slept at night while Gramps took the third bedroom. He called Mitch to his side, and they watched while Rachel laid the papers in a row across a blanket on the floor. He'd suggested that way earlier, so if the drug scent got on anything, it would only be the blanket.

She went through that same routine three times with a different set of papers before Mitch indicated the scent of drugs and barked. Rachel glanced in the direction of the bedrooms. "I'm not sure we won't wake them up if there's more than this one."

By the time Mitch had checked all the papers in the bag, Rachel had collected ten different sheets. "They're all different. A couple of time sheets for the boat crews. Some are shipping notices and a few are orders."

"The paper most likely was touched by someone who had been handling drugs, and some of those sheets were contaminated by the original one or two."

"Which doesn't narrow it down a lot. I'll write these down, and then we can look at the boats in the harbor for the past week since all these papers are from that time frame." Rachel jotted down the information and then collected everything and stuck it in the canvas bag. "I feel like a criminal having to sneak these in and out of the fishery."

"If something fishy is going on, we need to find out and let Randall know. I don't want to accuse anyone without evidence, but the police chief did say he needed my help. They're shorthanded."

Rachel chuckled. "Definitely something fishy is going on. That's the nature of the business." She sat next to Jake on the couch. "Here is the list of boats in the harbor the past week with when they came and when they left, if they're gone."

Jake lounged back and read the forty names. "Is anyone who works for the fishery not on this list because they've been out over a week?"

Rachel leaned toward him and reread the list. "There are three due back soon. There are some boats in the harbor that have nothing to do with the fishery."

The apple scent from her shampoo teased his nostrils. He'd come to associate that smell with warmth and caring. She'd always had a calming effect on him. "We'll concentrate on the boats that work for the company. Let me see the list of contaminated sheets."

She handed it to him. "They are all from people on the list of boats in the harbor, but I would expect that. So how does this help us?"

"Not sure yet. I'm going to start taking Mitch for walks on the pier and see if anything catches his attention. I'll concentrate on the four boats on this second list. Who handles the crew time sheets?"

"Everyone writes down their own hours, then the captain verifies it and turns it in. I can't see the Blue Runner having anything to do with Aunt Betty's death. They were out of the harbor on Friday and Saturday. The other three were tied up in their slips."

"I can't rule them out concerning the drugs, but you're right about Aunt Betty's death. So tell me about Tundra King, Alaskan King and Sundance." The brush of her arm against his threatened to steal his concentration on the task at hand.

"Tundra King and Alaskan King are owned by the company. As I told you before, the Alaskan King is a new trawler. Captain Martin of the Sundance sells his catches to the fishery."

While he looked over the lists, Jake asked, "Who is in port right now?"

"Alaskan King and the Blue Runner. Tundra King left today and Sundance is due back tomorrow. We're closed for two weeks during the holidays, then we start back up with crabbing. What do you want me to do to help?"

He dipped his head and turned toward her, her glance trapping him in a snare. For a moment he didn't say anything until she dropped her gaze to the papers. "You've done it. Leave the rest to me. This is my job."

"But you don't have access to the fishery like I do."

After nearly losing her in the fire, he didn't want to take the risk. "I'll find a way. Remember Sean and I were good friends in high school, and I was over in the processing center with him today before we went to lunch. Gramps and I know many of the men who work there."

"I thought we were in this together. I want to find who did this to Aunt Betty. She was family. She doesn't deserve this."

*And I want to keep you safe.* If anything happened to her…he shuddered at the thought. "We're a team. We've always been one."

"But that wasn't enough to keep you here or let me know about the injury you suffered in August until much later." Rachel pushed to her feet and walked to the Christmas tree. After turning off the lights, she shut the drapes. "I have to be at work by seven thirty. Good night." She started for the hallway.

"Rachel," Jake called out and rose. When she stopped, he bridged the distance between them. "I'm sorry. I promise I'll be around so much in the future you're going to get tired of me, but my job is in Anchorage. I make a difference. I'm good at working with a K-9."

She spun around, her teeth digging into her lower lip. She did that when she wanted to remain quiet and was fighting the urge to talk.

"I've seen Celeste on a number of occasions, and my life hasn't fallen apart. She doesn't have any power over me anymore."

She inched closer and lifted her hands to cup his jaw. "Good. I hated seeing what she did to you. I wish you'd come to that decision years ago."

"What can I say, I'm stubborn."

She leaned toward him and kissed his mouth

lightly, then dropped her arms to her sides and rushed from the living room.

His lips tingled from the contact with hers. Suddenly, he wanted more than just a brief kiss. He watched her disappear into her bedroom and wondered why in the world it had taken him so long to see her as more than a friend. He shook his head and pivoted. But that was crazy. Neither of them wanted a long-term commitment.

On Wednesday Rachel stood next to Jake. Halfway through the memorial service for Betty, she grasped his hand, needing that connection, or she might break down. Then her aunt would start crying, and she was to speak at the end.

When Aunt Linda finished paying tribute to Aunt Betty, the church choir sang "Amazing Grace" and then her aunt announced that after the Christmas tree lighting everyone was invited to come back to the hall for refreshments provided by the Port Aurora Community Church's women.

Jake bent to her ear and whispered, "Are you ready? Do you need to stay?"

His breath on her neck tickled, making her think about the kiss she'd given him the other day. She'd wanted more, but she was afraid of these feelings his presence was generating in her. She'd always thought they had been best friends, but now she wondered if she hadn't taken it further and felt rejected when he fell in love with Celeste instead of her.

"Rachel, are you okay?"

She closed her eyes for a few seconds. "I'm all right. Aunt Betty used to come with us to the ceremony at the harbor when all the lights were turned on officially. The part I love is the lights in the harbor are turned off for a few minutes while the mayor gives a little speech then flips the switch. Then for a while the only lights are on the Christmas tree. It's like a ray of hope at the end of the pier, that Port Aurora is welcoming any lost soul." And now someone had tainted their small town.

"I never thought of it like that. I see Gramps is with your aunt. If we're going to get a good place, we better leave."

"The best places are reserved for the children at the front. Remember when we would push our way through the crowd so we were in the first row?"

"Yes, but they always tolerated us doing that. Does the mayor still toss out candy to the kids?"

"Yes, and I wouldn't mind something chocolate right about now." When Rachel stepped outside, she lifted her hood since the wind off the water could be freezing cold.

"Remember that year the harbor iced over? Thankfully, that doesn't happen every year."

"But the water feels like it could turn to ice at any moment. I've never been into the polar bear plunge some people do."

Jake laughed. "Neither have I, but I have navigated some cold rivers and streams before that almost felt like that's what I was doing."

Again she felt like years of separation had slipped away, and their relationship had returned to what it was before Celeste. But he would be leaving again in a few weeks. Would he stay away as long as he had before? She had to remind herself even though he might come home two or three times a year, their friendship wouldn't be the same. She wished he would work for the Port Aurora Police Department like he had before going to Anchorage. What was the lure of a big city? A place with too many people and not enough open space wasn't for her.

Jake maneuvered them to where they could see the tree well but at the back of the crowd and off to the side on one of the docks. "So much for hurrying. We're going to be at the back, anyway. Want me to put you on my shoulders? Maybe the mayor will take pity on you and toss you a piece of chocolate."

"I know where there is some chocolate at Aunt Betty's reception afterward."

Jake saw Lawrence and Aunt Linda and waved to them. They headed in their direction.

"Being back here is probably the best since we have to get to the hall to serve the food and refreshments." Aunt Linda took the place next to Rachel while Lawrence and Jake began talking.

Then the lights in the harbor and surrounding area went out. With a cloudy night Rachel couldn't see anything around her. She touched her aunt beside her. "Now for the mayor's long-winded speech. It gets longer every year."

"That's because he's always running for mayor at any ceremony he officiates."

Someone moved into Rachel's faint line of sight, so she sidestepped a couple of feet away from her aunt and snuggled in her heavy parka. "When we get home a roaring fire in the fireplace would be great."

"I know what you mean," her aunt's voice came from the dark nearby.

Rachel opened her mouth to say something

to Aunt Linda when a large body rammed into her and she went flying backward…into the freezing water.

# SEVEN

When Rachel hit the frigid water, she gasped as if she'd been submerged in a bucket of ice. She plunged totally under, taking in a mouth full of salty water. Instinct kicked in, and she fought to the surface, her heavy parka like a boulder dragging her down.

*Have to scream. Only minutes before I begin shutting down.* The thought sent panic surging through her, and she thrashed, barely keeping her head above water.

*Calm down.*

In her mind she could hear Jake talking to her in a soothing voice. *Stay still. I'm coming.*

*No, don't. I can't lose you, too.* She tried to say those words aloud, but her heartbeat raced at a dizzying speed, and her body started shivering from head to toe.

* * *

Behind Jake, a woman screamed, the blood-curdling sound vying with a loud splash as if someone hit the water. He swung around, so dark he could only see about a foot in front of him.

He headed toward where Rachel was a few feet away. "Rachel, what's wrong?"

Linda used her cell phone like a flashlight and gasped. "Someone pushed her into the water!"

His heartbeat galloping, Jake quickened his step, removing his cell and using it to illuminate his path. "Gramps, we need light."

People around them began doing the same with their phones while he glimpsed his grandfather shoving his way through the crowd. The fear on Linda's face scared Jake. As he reached her, she grabbed his arm and pointed toward the water.

The faint light from their cells barely showed a head bobbing in the water, arms thrashing. Rachel looked so far away when in reality she wasn't.

"Stay calm. I'm coming." Struggling could make the situation a lot worse. The movement would lower her body temperature faster.

Jake searched the pier and saw a lifebuoy

against a piling. He rushed to it, grabbed it and hurried back. "Rachel, I'm going to toss this life buoy to you. Hold on and get as much of yourself above water as possible."

Coughing followed a weak, quavering voice saying, "I will."

Suddenly, the harbor lights flooded the area, and Jake could make out Rachel better as he threw the life buoy to her. She grasped it and hung on.

Now he had to get her out of the water—over four yards below the pier. Too bad it was low tide.

Tom appeared behind him. "My boat isn't far. I have a skiff on it. It would be easier to haul her out of the water from it."

He and Tom raced to the Blue Runner with a skiff attached. Tom lowered it to the water. Each minute they took, Rachel's body temperature was dropping. In less than fifteen minutes, hypothermia could set in. That didn't leave much time to get to her.

Bright light illuminated the harbor and hurt her eyes. Rachel closed them and tried to latch on to a single thought, but her mind raced with nonsense.

She couldn't feel her arms and legs. Were they moving? Shivers consumed her body.

The sound of concerned voices reached her. Jake? Aunt Linda?

*Help, Lord.*

A loud noise penetrated the haze that gripped her. She eased her eyes open, comforted to see she was still holding the life buoy. If she let go, she was sure she would sink to the bottom of the harbor. Then she saw a skiff coming toward her with Jake in the front of it.

"Hang on, Rachel. Almost there," he shouted over the racket of the motor.

She tried tightening her hold on the life preserver but couldn't feel if she had or not. It seemed like ice had replaced the marrow in her bones.

*Stay calm and still.* She repeated those words she remembered Lawrence telling her and Jake once about falling through the ice. Her eyelids slid closed again.

The sound of the motor stopped—nearby. But she couldn't find the strength to open her eyes.

"Rachel! Rachel!"

She turned her head slightly and looked at Jake leaning over the side of the boat. "You're here," she said while her teeth chattered so much she wasn't sure he heard her.

He scooped down and hooked his arms under hers, then lifted her from the water. The second she was in the skiff, it started moving toward a larger boat.

"You'll feel much better once you get out of your wet clothes." Jake used his body to block the wind that knifed through her while he stripped off her gloves and heavy parka and then wrapped her in a blanket. "This is only until Tom gets you back to the Blue Runner. I see your aunt. She'll help you then."

Rachel caught the gist of what he said, but pain took hold of her from her feet to her head. And cold still had its icy talon around her.

When they reached the Blue Runner, hands grabbed at her. She pushed them away and pressed herself closer to Jake. The memory slammed her. Someone had pushed her into the water. *Who?*

"I've got her." Jake swung her up into his embrace and leaped to the trawler.

The motion made her sick to her stomach. She buried her face against him. As he walked then descended some stairs, she knew she would be safe with him.

When he set her feet on the floor of the

boat, she began to sink down, but Jake's arm clamped around her and steadied her.

"Have her sit, then leave. I'll get her clothes off. I need a warm blanket. Some warm sweet tea," a familiar female voice said.

Rachel met her aunt's worried expression. "I'll be okay."

Aunt Linda helped her undress, then wrapped blankets around her. She towel-dried Rachel's wet hair and pulled a wool beanie down over her head, followed by a scarf around her neck. "Doc is on his way."

Even though her feet and hands tingled as though tiny needles were being stuck in her, Rachel hated Aunt Linda missing the rest of the evening's events held in Aunt Betty's honor. "I want you to go to the memorial service reception. I'm going to be fine. Doc said so. Tom, you loved Aunt Betty. You need to go and take my aunt and Lawrence." Rachel lay on a bunk bundled up like a baby with everyone standing around waiting for something to happen.

"I agree Linda and Tom need to attend, but I'm staying with Jake and Rachel. I'll keep watch. No one is gonna hurt Rachel." The fierce expression on Lawrence's face matched

Jake's earlier one when he had been determined to haul her out of the frigid water.

Her aunt and Tom looked at each other, then Tom replied, "I'm only going to be there an hour. Is that okay with you, Linda?" When her aunt nodded, Tom grabbed his heavy coat and shrugged into it. "Rachel, you need to stay on my boat and rest for the time being. When you think you are capable, you should get up and walk some. Get your blood pumping. I'm just thankful you were only in the water fifteen minutes. I've pulled a few guys from the Bering Sea and believe me it isn't fun. Ready, Linda?"

Her aunt leaned down and kissed Rachel's cheek. "Are you sure you're okay?"

"Believe me. The feeling is definitely returning to my limbs. I'm not shivering as much. Go."

Jake moved to Lawrence and murmured something to him. The older man frowned but gave a nod.

"I'm coming with you." Lawrence slipped into his parka.

After the trio left, Rachel peered at Jake, standing at the back door they'd left through, staring at the harbor through the window. She glimpsed the bright lights of the Christmas tree. They blended with the other illuminations on the pier. "The man who pushed me in was waiting for the right time. It would have been hard to get away unseen if the lights had been on at the harbor."

Jake turned, his forehead creased, the look in his eyes thoughtful. But she could see the worry in them.

"I'm fine now, Jake." She wasn't so sure an hour ago she could have said that.

He closed the space between them and sat in the chair next to the bunk. "You came close to dying for the second time in less than a week. I don't..." He cleared his throat. "I don't know what I would do if anything happened to you."

She brought her hand out from under the blankets and laid it over his, drawn to the warmth radiating from him. "Obviously, someone thinks I know what's going on, so we'll take precautions. They may be sending a message not to dig any deeper, which means we're on the right track. My aunt was murdered. Something bad is going down in the town I love. I can't ignore that."

"That's what I'm supposed to say. I'm a police officer. You aren't."

"But I'm in the middle of this, and that's not

going to change. We need to be sneakier. Don't give them anything to worry about."

One corner of his mouth quirked. "I think we're beyond that. You have to promise me you'll be careful wherever you go and to assess each situation as though someone was out to kill you."

"What did Chief Quay say about the incident?"

"One lady late to the lighting of the tree saw a tall man running away. Another felt a jostle as someone went through the crowd. Nothing clear-cut."

"What did you say to Lawrence?" Rachel finally realized that he had captured her free hand and had it cupped between his. She savored the warmth of his skin against hers.

"I want him to go Betty's reception because they were friends, and I also want him to listen to what people were talking about. Sometimes a person will witness a crime but not step forward because they're afraid. If there is a witness that saw something who isn't coming forward, maybe I can at least talk to him in private."

"Are you always thinking like a cop?"

He grinned. "Pretty much. Except if I get my hands on the guy who did this, I might forget

I'm a police officer and take matters into my own hands."

"In situations like this one and what happened with Betty, I find it difficult to forgive the person who caused them."

"I've continued to wrestle with that since I became a police officer. I haven't forgiven the bomber, and I don't know if I can. He hurt a lot of people and changed many lives—not for the better."

"How about your mother?"

His smile faded, and he released her hand, pulling back. "I didn't think much about her in Anchorage. I can't change the fact that she didn't want to be a mother. At least in your case it was your mom's new husband who didn't want children, and later she asked you if you wanted to come live with her."

"Only after she divorced and married husband number four. I think my mom leaving me with Aunt Linda was the best thing she could do for me. In her own way she loved me, but my aunt has really been my mother."

"So you've forgiven her?"

Rachel thought a moment, searching her heart to make sure of her answer. "Yes. I like the stability I've had here. This is home." *I wish you saw it that way.* The words were there in her mind, but she couldn't say them to him. Although both of their mothers left them in Port Aurora, his situation was much different, and he still hadn't dealt with it.

Jake rose. "Tom said to get you up and walking around. I don't want him to come back and have to tell him I didn't." He offered her his hand.

Again she put hers in his, and he helped her to stand. Her body ached, and her muscles were stiff, but she shed her blankets, wearing clothes borrowed from the general store. A chill hung in the cabin, even though the heater was on, but it was much warmer than outside in the cold and wind.

Jake retrieved his coat and slung it over her shoulders, then he held her arm and took a step. Once she began walking, she loosened up. She felt safe next to him. In less than a week she'd come to depend on him being in Port Aurora. She had to work on that because he was leaving at the end of the month, and she didn't want to go through the hurt she had when he left eight years ago.

"When they return, I want to go home. I can walk to the car now."

"But your shoes are still wet and all you

have are the socks from the general store. You can't walk. I'll carry you."

She started to protest, but he was right. And she knew she'd enjoy being in his arms. That thought surprised her, but her feelings for Jake had always been deep, so she shouldn't be. She cared about him beyond friendship, feelings that were doomed to cause nothing but heartache.

Rachel and Linda's house was quiet—too quiet for Jake. He sat up on the couch and swung his legs to the floor. He probably slept no more than three or four hours. He couldn't shake the image of Rachel bobbing in the harbor's ice-cold water. When he'd stuck his hand in the water to hoist her up into the skiff, he'd gotten enough of a feel of what she'd been in. Hypothermia could strike quick in Alaska.

He switched on a lamp and checked his watch. Five in the morning. He might as well get up and make the coffee and then use the time to go over what they knew so far about Betty's murder. What if he couldn't find the killer? How could he leave knowing Rachel was in danger? For that matter, Gramps and Linda? Worse, if a drug-smuggling ring was working out of Port Aurora, it would be a big blow to the town. If drugs were tied up in Betty's case, that heightened the danger even more. He would call a buddy he knew who was a state trooper and specialized in apprehending illegal drugs. Maybe he'd heard something.

Jake headed into the kitchen and put on a pot of coffee to brew. Then he began to pace while he waited for it to perk. An unsettling restlessness dominated him, and he didn't know if he would get a good night's sleep until the case was solved.

But he wasn't sure the feeling was totally caused by the murder. Ever since he'd returned to Port Aurora, he had been fighting mixed emotions. Being home was what he needed, and yet Celeste's appearance had churned up all he'd gone through years ago. He'd honestly thought he'd gotten over her, but maybe it was because he'd never really resolved things with her.

Last night Rachel had asked him about forgiving his mother. But it wasn't only her he needed to deal with, but Celeste, too. When he'd started dating her, he'd had such hopes that Celeste could banish the feelings of abandonment his mother had caused. Instead, she'd added to them. That was why he wouldn't commit to another.

"That coffee smells great."

Jake spun around and faced Rachel dressed in the same sweats from the night before. The color had returned to her cheeks, and as she walked into the kitchen, she wasn't stiff. Seeing her alive and all right was the most beautiful sight. "You should be sleeping."

"Then you shouldn't have made coffee. That's all that keeps me going some days."

"Me, too. Do you think it will wake up your aunt? I know she was really tired when she went to bed."

"She usually drinks tea, so it shouldn't. How about Lawrence?"

"Probably not, but if we fried bacon he would be in here instantly."

Rachel went to the cabinet and took two mugs from it. "That would draw me, too. That and baking bread. Maybe later I'll make some biscuits, bacon and gravy. I feel bad about staying home today."

"But according to your aunt, Brad was adamant you not come into work. I think he's right. You might be okay now, but your body went through an ordeal. I have a feeling you'll be taking a long nap by midmorning."

Rachel sat at the table. "Oh, you think so."

"Take it from me, I know a little about

traumas." Jake filled the mugs, then put her coffee in front of her and took the chair next to her.

"How long were you trapped in the debris?"

"They told me three hours before they dug me out. Part of that time I was unconscious. The worst thing was I couldn't get to Mitch, but I heard him whining. It broke my heart to listen. Maybe it was good I passed out. We both broke a leg. They could fix mine but not his."

Rachel looked around. "Where is Mitch?"

"Sleeping on the bed next to Gramps. He knows I won't let him, but Gramps did."

Rachel laughed. "I don't blame Mitch. I'd rather sleep there than on the floor."

"I brought his bedding."

"Not the same thing. I hope the couch isn't the reason you aren't sleeping."

The picture of Rachel trying to escape the fire followed by being in the water invaded his mind again. He couldn't lose her. "No, you're the reason."

"Me?" She pointed to herself. "I'm all right."

"Just to make sure, Doc is coming back today to check on you. Also, Randall will be coming."

Rachel took a sip of her drink. "How am

I supposed to rest with everyone parading through here?"

"Oh, I don't think that will be a problem. Your body will tell you. Take it from me. I had visions when I was in the hospital of being up and around, even going to work, within a month. As you see, that didn't happen. I still have a slight limp when I'm tired, and the weather can make my leg ache."

"I don't understand why you didn't want me to come to visit you then."

He thought back to those first few weeks and shook that image from his mind. "I didn't want you to see me bitter and angry. Especially at God. There were people still missing. I was trying to save others. Instead, I ended up hurt. Mitch did, too."

"It's hard not to feel that way, but everything happens for a reason. We don't always know what it is. Faith is what gets us through it."

"You sound like Gramps. He wouldn't let me wallow for long."

"Did they find the missing people?"

"One was found alive, but the other was dead." Jake finished off his last few sips of the lukewarm coffee. "So what are you going to do on your day off?"

One of her eyebrows hiked up. “Day off? Didn’t you remind me that I needed to rest?”

“Good. Just checking to make sure you know what you should do. I thought I might return to find you gone and taking your car to work. More than ever I need to be with you. I don’t want to go through a third attempt on your life.”

“And neither do I.” She rose. “Do you want some more coffee?”

He came to his feet and put his hands on her shoulders. “What part of resting did you not get? I can refill our cups.”

“I hope Lawrence was as relentless with you as you are with me.”

The laughter in her gaze twisted the knot in his gut that had yet to unravel from the events of the evening before. It transformed her pretty face into a beautiful one and made her brown eyes come to life. He sometimes felt trapped by them, as he was now.

He almost lost her last night. For a moment a bone-cold chill encased him. He cradled her head and leaned toward her lips. When his mouth covered hers, for the first time in a long while, he felt at peace.

# EIGHT

On Friday Rachel stared out the window of her Jeep as Jake drove her to work. The snow-layered landscape passed by, but she really wasn't seeing the beauty before her. Most of her thoughts for the past day had been centered on the kiss Jake gave her yesterday morning. He had taken her by surprise—a very pleasant one, and afterward she'd walked around the house in a daze. She wanted him to kiss her again, and yet she didn't. He didn't want to make a long-term commitment to a woman—not after his mother and Celeste—but that was the only kind she would have, and there was no way to guarantee that.

"Rachel, we're here." Jake cut into her musing with Mitch barking from the backseat.

She blinked and focused on the fishery headquarters in front of the car. "Sorry, I was thinking."

"Dangerous. Aren't you sick of the case after spending most of yesterday going over and over what little we know?"

"Solving a crime is different than on TV. They have it done in an hour, and it looks so easy, especially when the suspect confesses."

Jake laughed, a deep belly kind. "If only that were the case. My detective friend, Thomas, would actually have normal hours if it were."

She loved hearing him laugh like that. She'd gotten the impression he hadn't done much of that in the past four months. "Is he the guy you're going to call today?"

"No, he works for the Anchorage Police Department. He worked on the bomber case. I don't think he had a life during that time. Actually, most police officers didn't. A lot were working double shifts and overtime."

"Are you going to stop in to see Chief Quay?"

"Maybe, if my walk on the pier proves profitable."

"Who knows what kind of dog Mitch is?"

"A few people here in Port Aurora—Randall, Gramps, your aunt. I don't think anyone else."

"With his missing limb, that ought to throw anyone off."

Jake's eyes widened. "I never thought that his injury would be a blessing, but you're right. What boats are coming in today?"

"Only two that the company owns, the Alaskan King and Tundra King. There may be one other that contracts with the fishery. They should be in before dusk."

"I'll probably wait until after lunch to take a walk with Mitch on the pier. I'll pick you up, and we can go to the café at twelve."

"You don't have to escort me to lunch. This is your vacation. You should spend some time with your grandfather."

"We did, yesterday. This morning I'm going to observe the fishery operations. Gramps is coming into town in a couple of hours to explain what's going on in each area. His friend who owns the bait shop near the harbor is visiting relatives in the lower forty-eight. We're going to use that as our base of operation. It has windows on three sides, so we'll be able to see most of the fishery and harbor."

"But what about the inside of the fishery?"

"I want to narrow down my search. If I went everywhere, that would make someone suspicious with all that's happened so far. Gramps might take Mitch with him to visit a friend. I can also go to the processing center. After lunch the other day, Sean and I talked about getting together."

"And I can go anywhere."

"No. You are *not* to do anything. Someone has gone after you two times. Stay in your office."

"But—"

"There's no but to it. Stay or I'm going to glue myself to you."

Rachel bit her bottom lip rather than protest. She had to do her job, or that would raise more questions and suspicions. "If I go anywhere in the fishery, it will be during the daylight hours."

His glare bored into her. "I'm probably going to have to spend all my time at the bait shop just keeping an eye on you gallivanting around the fishery and harbor. I'll bring you coffee from the café before I head that way."

"Thanks. I'd better go. I'm already late." Rachel climbed from her Jeep and hurried toward the building. Since they'd gotten a late start, she didn't have the time to stop at the café before work, so she would appreciate the coffee later.

Inside, Rachel stashed her purse in a locked drawer of her desk, then proceeded to Brad's office to get his final amounts for the employee bonuses going out today. He'd been dragging his feet for some reason. His secretary was gone, so Rachel headed toward his door. It stood slightly ajar, and she lifted her hand to knock.

"The shipment will be ready to go on time," Sean said in his deeply raspy voice. "Even with holiday leave coming up, we'll finish processing the Tundra King and Alaskan King's catches that are coming in today. It sounds like they had a good haul. I understand there will be a couple of boats going out during the two weeks most are on vacation. I can run a skeleton crew during that time. There are some without families that don't care. Now that we've expanded we should look at running all the way through December, except for Christmas and Christmas Eve."

"I don't want to change that policy. I've already cut down the time we're gone drastically to accommodate the expansion. There's more to life than work."

"But Ivan and I can handle..."

Rachel backed away, not wanting to eavesdrop. Brad was in a meeting with Sean. She'd talk with her employer later today about the bonuses. As she turned to leave, she came face-to-face with Eva Cohen, Brad's secretary and the wife of the Tundra King's captain. The older woman's shoulders were thrust back, and she was so stiff that a light breeze could snap her in two.

"What are you doing?" The secretary's terse tone cut through Rachel.

"Brad and I are supposed to speak sometime this morning. I thought I would catch him before the day starts, but he's busy, so I'll come back."

"I'll inform *Mr. Howard* you are at work, and let you know when he can see you." Mrs. Cohen raised her chin and peered at Rachel from the bottom of her glasses. "He's a busy man, and you should always call ahead to see if he's available."

In the past, Brad had an open-door policy, but everything changed with Mrs. Cohen's arrival last summer. She guarded access to him like a mama bear did her cubs. "I'll try to remember that," she muttered, clenching her hands as she left and hurried back to her office.

Brad had better let her know about the bonuses this morning. She would be passing out the checks early since most of the people went on vacation after Wednesday. That was supposed to be everyone's last day until after the New Year. But according to Sean, there would be a skeleton crew working over part of the holidays, at least if he had his way. Since when? Why didn't anyone tell her? She would have to note that so she could pay them at the end of the month.

She worked on the early checks for next week and would add the bonuses in when her employer let her know. When someone cleared their throat, she looked up and found Jake, leaning against her doorjamb, a paper coffee cup in each hand.

"I come bearing gifts." Jake walked to her desk and set the drinks on it, then went back out into the hallway and brought in a sack with the scent of freshly baked glazed donuts, something she loved from the café but rarely indulged in. "I figure you would be starved with only a piece of toast for breakfast."

"You must have heard my stomach rumbling all the way to the café. Where's Lawrence?"

"He went on to the bait shop. I told him I wouldn't be long, and he said for me to take my time."

"Then he has Mitch."

"Yep. I think Mitch has bonded with Gramps. It must be the soft bed he gets to sleep in. Could you see me with two big dogs trying to sleep in a double bed? I'd probably end up on the floor while they ruled the bed."

"Mitch has worked hard. He deserves a few luxuries."

Jake chuckled. "My dog has gotten to you, too."

Rachel dug into the sack and pulled out one fluffy donut, dripping with glaze. "He's a sweetie."

"Shh. Don't say that to him. He may be officially retired, but I intend at least to keep him involved in search-and-rescue missions where he doesn't have to chase after bad guys."

Jake took the chair in front of her desk and plucked a donut from the bag. "I brought you two. I know how much you love them."

"You didn't eat much more than I did this morning."

"But I already had two donuts with Gramps."

"So where's my third one?"

He smiled from ear to ear. "I told Gramps you would say something like that." He rose and went into the hallway again. A half a minute later he set another sack on her desk.

Her eyes grew round. "I was half kidding. I can't eat three right now."

Jake retook his seat. "Save it for later and have a midafternoon treat."

"I overheard an interesting conversation—"

Jake put his forefinger over his mouth.

That was when she heard footsteps coming down the hall. She took a bite of her donut, then a sip of her coffee.

Brad poked his head around the door frame. "I thought I heard voices. It's good to see you again, Jake." Her employer came into her office and passed her a sheet of paper. "Those are the amounts for the bonuses according to what they do. I've singled out a few that have gone above and beyond their duties to see the fishery do well this year."

"Thanks. I wanted to work on payroll today because there is paperwork that needs to be done by the end of the year before I go on vacation."

Brad started for the door and glanced back. "By the way, Mrs. Cohen is right. Call before you come to the office. That way you don't waste your time. Have a good weekend."

As the sound of the footsteps receded, Jake said, "Tell me at lunch. We're going to have a picnic at the bait shop. I'll stop by and get you."

"You don't have—"

"When are you going to learn not to argue with me?"

"Probably never," she said with a laugh.

"See you at twelve."

When Jake left, she sipped her coffee and nibbled on the donut while looking over the list of bonuses. She stared at the amount for her and nearly dropped the sheet of paper. One month's salary! Twice as much as most of the people at the fishery. Why? She hadn't worked any harder than the others. She needed to check with Brad. That he hadn't added an extra zero by mistake.

She started to get up and head for his office when she remembered what her employer said right before he left. Instead, she picked up her phone and called him.

"Mr. Howard's office, Mrs. Cohen speaking."

Just to irritate the prim and proper secretary, Rachel said, "Eva, this is Rachel. I need to talk with Brad about the list he gave me a few minutes ago."

"Just a minute." A hard edge sharpened each word.

A long pause and Brad answered his phone. "Is there a problem, Rachel?"

"No, but I'm confused about my bonus numbers. You're giving me a month's salary instead of two weeks' pay."

"You're important to this fishery, and this

company is vital to the economy of Port Aurora. I'd hate to think what would happen if the company went under."

"Okay." She drew that word out; for some reason it wasn't really okay. "Thank you, Brad."

"You're welcome. Have a nice weekend." Then he hung up.

Rachel started when she heard a click on the phone. Was Mrs. Cohen listening to our conversation? Why would she? Should she tell Brad? But she really didn't know. Maybe she had imagined it.

Her eyes glued to the paper before her, she stared at the thousands of dollars she would receive.

Why did she feel she was being paid off?

When Jake arrived at Rachel's office at twelve, he found her prowling her domain as though restless energy had been bottled up in her and she was trying to release it. He took one look at her face and knew something was wrong. He gave her a quizzical look.

"Later. At lunch."

Not a word was spoken until they had walked away from the building. "Okay, what's wrong?" Jake asked, wondering if Rachel had done any work since he'd left her that morning.

She told him about the bonus that was two or three times more than she ever had received. "Plus, I think Brad's secretary, Mrs. Cohen, might have been listening to my conversation with him."

"Why would she do that?" Jake asked, making a note to investigate this woman.

"If I didn't know better, I would think she ran this place. Everything has to go through her to Brad. It was never like that before she came."

"Maybe she does. How did she get the job?"

"When her husband was hired as the captain of the Tundra King, she was given the job as Brad's secretary shortly afterward. Brad's previous one got another offer and moved away. It happened fast, and I guess Brad was grateful that Mrs. Cohen could fill in quickly. Celeste did the job temporarily until Mrs. Cohen came. Celeste left it a mess, so I can understand Brad's desire to keep Mrs. Cohen happy, but still..." Rachel twisted her mouth as she did when she was in deep thought. "Do you think Mrs. Cohen might be involved in what's going on?"

"I'm suspecting everyone until proven otherwise. If drug smuggling is taking place, we're dealing with ruthless people." Jake scanned the surroundings, then opened the door to the bait shop.

"All I have to do is think about Aunt Betty to know what kind of people they are." Rachel went inside first, greeting Gramps and Mitch.

"Anything happen while I was gone?" Jake asked his grandfather while rubbing his dog's back.

"The Alaskan King is unloading their catch." Gramps stepped away from the window that afforded a great view of the harbor and passed the binoculars to Jake. "It looks like the Tundra King is a few miles out so all the trawlers have returned. They'll be either shutting down or slowing way down until the first of the year."

Rachel frowned. "That may make it harder to find out what's going on if no drugs are coming through the fishery."

"Not necessarily. The scent of drugs will stay on an object for a while. Without so many people around, I might be able to investigate with Mitch inside the buildings, but because I'm a law-enforcement officer, our search has to be able to hold up in court."

"In plain sight?" Rachel asked as she stared out the window facing the processing center.

Jake lifted the binoculars to his eyes. "Yes, unless we get a warrant, which will need evidence of probable cause. We think someone is touching the drugs, testing or cutting them, to the point that the scent ended up on your paperwork, but that won't be enough to convince a judge."

Rachel's forehead furrowed. "Not even because Mitch discovered it? He's a drug dog."

"We need to search everywhere because we don't know what's going on, so no. We'll have to have more evidence. If we went to a judge now with what little we know, it would get out what our intention is, and the smuggling ring would shut down until we go away."

"This operation must involve more than a few people? These are people who have lived here and been our friends." His shoulders slumped, Gramps shuffled to the lunch sack and laid out the containers and wrapped sandwiches on the counter.

"Not all of them, Lawrence. We've had an influx of new people due to the expansion at the fishery. Many have been here less than a year."

"Yeah, but the ones in a position of authority are people from Port Aurora except Ivan Verdin. Could this go on without their knowledge?" Gramps took a bite of his fish sandwich, then drained the last of an old cup of coffee.

"My friend in state police is coming the first of next week. We'll gather what information we can and give it to him."

"But what about Aunt Betty's murderer? What if her death had nothing to do with the suspicious stuff going on at the fishery?" Rachel brought Jake his lunch while he stood guard at the window.

"I think they are tied together. Why else would someone have murdered her? She could have taken some pictures that showed something. Maybe the intruders who searched her house took the photos. We may never know, but she must have made someone very uncomfortable for them to risk killing her." Jake's gaze seized hers and held it. "You said that she was afraid. What made her act like that? Most likely, she stumbled upon something to do with the drug smuggling."

"If some people at the fishery are involved, how far is their reach in Port Aurora? Remember, Aunt Betty was interested in talking to you because you were a police officer.

Why didn't she go to the police here?" Rachel sat on a tall stool at the window with a view of the processing center. "What if she wandered around where she worked and discovered something? The catches are processed, then boxed up and shipped out."

"Who handles the boxing and shipping at the fishery?" Jake leaned closer to the window where a few of the slats in the blinds opened at a slant, while the rest were closed.

"Ivan Verdin, another transplant from Seattle, runs the shipping warehouse." Rachel popped a couple of chips into her mouth.

"Have I met him?" There was a time Jake knew everyone who worked at the fishery because Gramps used to do Sean's job. This visit had shown him how much he'd lost touch with the town he grew up in.

"Maybe. I can pull up a picture of him on my computer at my office."

"When I walk you back, I need you to do that. I want to know what all the players in this look like."

"I'll take over watching, Jake. Enjoy your lunch with Rachel," his grandfather murmured, too low for her to hear.

"Don't go there, Gramps." But Jake took him up on the offer. He'd rediscovered how much he loved Rachel's company and planned to enjoy it until he had to return to Anchorage. Jake sat on the other side of the counter from her and plopped his sandwich on the glass top. "I forgot to ask you if you like their fish sandwich."

"It's good. Really nothing at the café is bad."

"At least that's one thing that hasn't changed."

"We have gone through a lot of changes in the past year. If you'd come back this time last year, it wouldn't have been that different."

"When you think of your hometown, you always remember how it was when you were living there. I'm glad you haven't changed. There is one constant in Port Aurora—well, two with Gramps."

"Do you feel you've changed?"

He nodded. "I'm not naive anymore. Growing up here sheltered me from a lot of evil in this world."

"But you were a police officer here, too."

"Not the same thing."

"Are you happy in Anchorage?"

He didn't have a ready answer for her because he'd been avoiding asking himself that question. But if he said yes, he would be admitting it out loud. But he couldn't say no, either. So much had happened in the past four months. It might be different in another four. "I don't know."

Her forehead scrunched, and she pressed her lips together—lips he would like to kiss again and again. "That in itself tells me a lot. You are either happy or not."

"Not everything is black-and-white. In fact, most things aren't."

She finished her sandwich, then said, "I realize you were in the hospital for a couple of weeks and have faced a long rehabilitation, but—"

"Okay, I was fine until I came home. I'd forgotten how much this place meant to me. I promise you I'll come home more from now on."

"Alaskan King is still unloading. Tundra King has come into the harbor. It will be docking soon. I think this is a good time to go for a walk, Jake."

He looked at Gramps. "You're right. I guess it's back to surveillance mode. I'll walk you to your office, then I need to take Mitch on a hunt. Afterward, I'll stop to talk to Charlie. As harbormaster, he might have seen something and not realized it."

"Charlie is a good friend, but son, I wouldn't

trust anyone, not even Randall after all that has happened."

Jake rose and grabbed his dog's leash. Mitch immediately climbed to his feet, but not quite as quickly as he used to, which brought sorrow to Jake. "Let's go, Rachel. This may be the last time for a while that a boat is returning."

"So you think if there are drugs going through the fishery, they're coming in by boat?" Rachel headed for the exit.

"It's the most logical answer. One or more of the trawlers could be meeting another boat in the Bering Sea. US ships aren't the only ones there, and the Coast Guard can only patrol so much area at a time."

"I know."

Five minutes later Jake entered Rachel's office and closed the door. He didn't want someone overhearing them as she pulled up Verdin's photo. "You should lock your door every time you leave during the day."

"The important file cabinets are locked, so I only lock the door when I leave at night."

"Still, I would feel better."

"Okay." She sat behind the computer and brought up a list of personnel. She clicked on Verdin's folder, and his picture popped up on the screen.

"I've seen him. Last Saturday he was two people back from me while I was talking with Sean, so Verdin could have overheard."

"When you have time, you should wade through everyone's picture on here."

"Will it seem strange you are accessing those files?"

"I do from time to time. Generally not all at once, but it would be good to know who else was at the general store that morning."

"Then I'll be back after my stroll around the harbor."

Jake left and made his way down the incline to the pier. He gave Mitch the command to search for drugs, then strolled the length to the right, also going down the docks attached to the pier where the boats were moored. When he saw Tom, he waved and stopped to talk for a few minutes, while keeping an eye on the activity by the pier that ended at the processing and shipping buildings.

"So Rachel is at work today?" Tom asked, winding a long length of rope.

"Yes. It was all I could do to keep her home yesterday, but by the middle of the day she was glad she didn't come in. She took a three-hour nap."

"The cold water saps your strength. I'm just glad she's all right."

Jake gestured toward the two boats tied up. "It looks like the Alaskan King is finishing unloading. They must have had a big catch. They've been at it for quite a while."

"Yeah. That's always good for business."

"I think I'll take a closer look. I see Sean with someone else on the pier, supervising the unloading."

"That's Ivan Verdin. He oversees the shipping department."

"I haven't met him yet. Now's a good time to." Jake strode away.

Five minutes later Jake slowed his gait and headed toward Sean and Ivan, who stood holding clipboards, talking.

"Hi, Sean. I'm glad I caught you. I was going to stop by your office and see if you would like to go to the Harbor Bar and Grill this evening. We haven't had much time to catch up."

His friend glanced at Ivan, then shifted toward Jake. "That sounds nice. Have you met Ivan Verdin? He manages our growing shipping department. Ivan, this is Jake Nichols. We hung around together when we were teens."

Jake shook the man's gloved hand. "Nice to meet you. How long have you been in Port

Aurora?" he asked, although he already knew the answer.

"Since June. I'll be right back. I need to talk to the captain of the Alaskan King."

When the tall, thin man left, Sean watched him walk away while Jake tried to see what was on his clipboard, but it was clasped against his coat. "I'm surprised Brad didn't promote within the workers at the fishery. That's what he did for you and Rachel."

"Ivan comes with experience from another fishery in Seattle. He's had great ideas about the packaging and shipping."

"So he's from Seattle like Brad's new partner?"

Sean's eyes popped wide. "I guess he is. I never thought about it."

"Want to give me a tour of this part of the new fishery?"

"I wish I could. I'm going to be really busy for the next few hours."

Jake had given Mitch a long leash, and he'd gone as far as he could, sniffing everything around him. Jake caught Ivan glancing back at him, a scowl on his face. This wasn't the time to look around. "See you at six at the grill."

Jake didn't go to the bait shop because when he looked back a couple of times, he found

Ivan watching him. Jake headed to Rachel's office to go through the rest of the employee files. He'd have Gramps take Rachel and Mitch home tonight while he met his friend to pump him for information.

Almost nine o'clock and the Harbor Bar and Grill was finally beginning to thin out. Jake had drunk three cups of coffee while Sean had ordered one beer after another. He'd never seen his friend drink so much alcohol. Thankfully, he lived near the harbor so he could walk to and from his job. What had made Sean change? When other teens were experimenting with alcohol, Sean never had. He prayed that Sean wasn't involved in the drug smuggling. The guy he grew up with wouldn't have been.

"I'm going to have to head home," Jake said when the bartender rang a boat bell nine times.

"Don't. We haven't had a chance to talk about your job. I think you know everything that has gone on since you left, but you're awfully closemouthed about Anchorage." Sean slurped the last of his drink and set the mug on the table with a loud thud.

"There's little to tell."

"You were injured searching a bombed building. What about that?"

He hated talking about it, but he didn't say that to Sean. Instead, he replied, "We'll get together again, and I'll tell you all the gory details. Let me drop you off at your house before I head home."

Sean waved his hand in the air. "I'm not drunk. I can walk. You go on and leave."

"I don't mind taking you home."

"I know. But I'm gonna stick around and escort our waitress Bev home. She lives down the street from me." He tapped his temple. "I've got my eye on her. She's interested in me."

Reluctantly, Jake left the restaurant and limped to Gramps's SUV. It was long days like this one that reinforced he'd been injured only four months ago and nearly died. Sean could take care of himself.

He climbed in and started the car. He hadn't learned much tonight, but he did get the feeling Sean really didn't care for Ivan and that the man was difficult to work with.

After looking through the photos of the employees, Jake couldn't remember anyone else that stood out to him that Saturday at the general store. What if one of the police officers was involved? After all, he'd been talking with Randall about where else he was going on that day. They might have alerted the arsonists to go to Betty's cabin. So many questions, so few answers.

The roads were much better since the last snowfall, but Jake focused his full attention on the highway. In the dark, he didn't have a lot of time to react if there was a slick spot that had developed that day.

In the distance across a field, he spied the Christmas lights on Linda's house. That meant he was only a mile away. Suddenly, someone stepped out of the brush on the side of the road and aimed a rifle at Jake.

# NINE

Rachel circled the living room for the tenth time and glanced at her watch. Nine thirty. Where was Jake? She paused at the front window and stared into the night, hoping to see two headlights coming. Nothing but darkness.

Mitch came up beside her and sat, looking up at her.

"I know, boy. Something doesn't feel right. He should have been home by now."

"Child, my grandson can take care of himself. He was meeting with Sean. You three used to hang out together in high school. You know how those two will get to talking and forget the time."

"You're right. But if anything happened to him because of me, I don't know what..." Emotions crowded into her throat, stopping her words. She swallowed hard but couldn't continue. She didn't want to lose him again, especially now that he was back in her life. This time she hoped he would visit Port Aurora more often, and she would go to Anchorage to see him. And maybe in time they—

Lawrence wedged himself between the Christmas tree and her. "I know how you feel. You love him."

"Of course I love him. He's my best friend. I'm not letting him disappear from my life for the next eight years." He'd hurt her when he'd left and she'd mostly stayed away, nursing her wounds.

Lawrence angled his head toward her. "I think it's more than friendship, but you two are too busy running away from commitment to see it."

Was that true? In the past week so many feelings had surfaced. Anger at him for keeping his distance. Relief that he was here to help with Aunt Betty's case. And then she thought of the kiss they'd shared—not anything like two good friends would. But Lawrence had a point. They both had commitment issues.

"Tell you what, Rachel. We'll give him another half an hour, and then I'll drive you to town. We'll take Mitch and hunt him down."

"He's at the Harbor Bar and Grill. I could call them and see if he's still there."

"Give him some time. I know a lot has been happening in Port Aurora, but the town is still essentially the same."

She turned toward Lawrence. "Is it? This past year we have added over five hundred to our population. With growth can come more crime, and if there is drug smuggling going down in the town, then it will only get worse."

"We still don't know that for sure."

"Both Jake and I strongly suspect it. We'll find the evidence to prove it if it's there. We can't ignore the scent of drugs on those papers in my office."

"Let me call the grill." Lawrence covered the space to the phone sitting on an end table in the living room, and dialed the number.

Rachel went back to her vigilance at the window. *Is this the way wives of police officers are when their husbands are late?*

Lawrence hung up and approached Rachel. "He's been gone for over half an hour. We're less than fifteen minutes from town."

"Then we have to go out looking for him." She headed for her purse and snatched up her keys to the Jeep.

A shot rang out, and the bullet hit the SUV's windshield. Jake ducked, and the car swerved toward the shooter. Another blast pierced a second hole into the glass, followed by a third.

Jake steered blind with one hand while fumbling for the glove compartment where his gun was. He grasped it as the SUV went into a spin. He rose, catching a glimpse of a figure fleeing right before Jake crashed into the thicket at the side of the road, the airbag exploding against his chest.

The hard impact into the ditch tossed him back then forward. A fine white powder choked him, and he coughed. Stunned and pinned against the seat, he closed his eyes to still the swirling sensation.

For a few seconds he couldn't remember what happened, then it all slammed back into his mind. As he shoved at the deflated airbag, he searched for his seat belt release. He pushed down on it.

*It's stuck.*

He fought rising panic, sucking in shallow gasps. Scenes from the bombing threatened to overtake his senses. Then he felt his weapon still clutched in his hand. Even if the man came to finish him off, he could protect himself. He jammed his thumb against the release once. Twice. Finally, the latch popped out, and the strap slackened across his chest.

His heartbeat racing, he began dragging in deeper breaths and searching the terrain around him. His headlights gave off illumination, enough that he didn't think the assailant was near. But how long would he remain away?

After he retrieved the flashlight in the glove compartment, Jake groped for the car handle, found it and shoved the door open. It creaked. The sound seemed to magnify and echo through the air, sending out a signal he was getting out of the car. All he had was a foot to squeeze out of the SUV. He pushed on the door, but it wouldn't budge any more.

After wiggling out of his bulky overcoat, he transferred his Glock to his left hand and clutched the parka in his right one. When he sucked in his breath, his bruised body protested. He gritted his teeth and squirmed out of the car.

When he stood, his legs started to give way. He gripped the door, leaning into it as he got his bearings. Then he noticed the cold boring into him and remembered to put on his coat.

He didn't want to stay around the SUV or walk home using the road. If the assailant came back, he would easily find him. He started across the field, using the lights in the distance as his guide to his destination. It had been years since he had walked over this ground. He tried to remember what obstacles were in his path.

Trudging slowly through the snow, he would head behind Betty's house and avoid the woods near where she'd lived. It would be a little longer but safer. He didn't want to use his flashlight unless absolutely necessary. If his assailant was looking for him, he wasn't going to make it easy.

The wind whipping across the flatland drove the cold deeper into him. Every sound heightened his alertness. About halfway home, Jake paused, turned his back to the wind and inhaled frigid air. His healing leg throbbed. His knee must have hit against the console. Every muscle screamed for him to sit and rest, but after a minute he scanned his dark-shrouded surroundings, then kept going toward the Christmas lights. The first thing he would do when he reached Linda's house was kiss them for stringing so many.

Then in the distance to his left came the sound of howls. A pack of wolves. He pressed on, trying to increase his speed to keep distance between them, but each time he lifted his leg out of the foot-deep snow, his steps shortened.

The howling continued. Jake's grip tightened around the gun handle. He pushed himself even more. Out of the corner of his eye, he saw a movement, but he couldn't tell what was there. From the well of what energy was left, he poured everything into his speed.

Suddenly, the ground beneath him fell away, and he tumbled downward.

"That's your car!" Rachel pointed toward the Jeep's front windshield. "He's been in a wreck." The words rushed out so fast she could hardly understand herself.

Heartbeat pounding against her rib cage, Rachel pulled over to the side of the road and put the Jeep's flashers on while Lawrence hopped from the car. They both converged on the driver's-side door, the headlights from her Jeep glowing into the SUV's dark interior.

Rachel straightened and turned toward Lawrence. "He's gone. I didn't see him walking home."

He leaned around her and examined the front seat. When he lifted his head toward the windshield, he tensed.

Slightly behind him, Rachel asked, "What's wrong?"

"There are three bullet holes in the windshield."

Rachel squeezed around Lawrence and bent

forward, glancing at the holes then the seat. "I don't see any blood. The keys are gone. Maybe he's okay, and we just missed him on the road." But as she said that, she didn't believe it.

Lawrence rounded the back of his car and opened the passenger door, then checked the glove compartment. "The flashlight is gone. Do you have one in your car?"

"Yes, the same place."

While Lawrence retrieved it, Rachel inspected the ground illuminated by the Jeep lights. "There are a lot of footprints here. I'm not sure which ones are ours."

Lawrence shone the flashlight a few feet from the SUV where there were two sets, not theirs. "There was someone else here. No doubt the shooter. One of these went southwest toward town and the other into the field."

Rachel followed the footsteps leading to a huge meadow near her house with the woods bordering part of it. "All I see is our Christmas lights. Nothing like a flashlight."

"Maybe that's why he went that way. It's the shortest way to our houses."

"What if he's hurt?" Rachel pointed to the tracks. "He's dragging the leg he injured in Anchorage. Isn't that what it looks like?"

Lawrence focused the flashlight on the drag

marks in the snow. "He crashed into the side of the ditch. He was going fast enough for the air bags to deploy. At the least he would have some bumps and bruises."

"Then we need to follow the tracks. What if he hit his head and isn't fully himself? He could have internal bleeding or..." Her throat jammed closed. She fought the tears welling inside her.

"He's a survivor. It was hours before he was safely rescued from the building rubble. He made it."

He had to be okay. He was hurt because of her. *Please, Lord, be with him. Show us where he is.*

Lawrence went first, illuminating the path, while Rachel trailed close behind him.

After walking ten minutes, she said, "Shine the light toward my house. We might catch his silhouette." She *needed* to see he was all right.

But when Lawrence swept the flashlight across the meadow, no one was there. Rachel's heart sank. "We've got to keep going. He may be in trouble."

Jake's feet went out from under him, and he slid downward. He slammed against the bottom of a snow-crusted crevice, his body wedged between the narrow walls. Pinned down. Stuck.

The only thing he could move was his right arm. His left one was trapped between his chest and the jagged stone. His weapon had jerked from his fingers as he fell, but lay within reach of his good arm.

He switched on his flashlight to see if he could figure a way out of the crevice. On both sides of him the walls were closer together. Until he'd fallen into the gap, he'd forgotten about there being a few in this meadow. He could have avoided or stepped over if he'd seen the fissure in time.

He turned off his light. He didn't want to call attention to his location. Hopefully, Gramps would find his SUV and figure out where he was going before anyone else. This was a time he was glad his grandfather was an expert shot, having been a sniper in the US Marines. He should be able to take care of himself if his assailant returned.

Since he couldn't see the wolves getting at him, all he had to worry about now was keeping himself warm when he could hardly move his limbs. The wind whipping through the crevice cut right through him. With his free hand, he pulled his hood, bunched around his neck, over his beanie. Occasionally, he stomped his feet and moved his right arm to keep the blood circulating, but the sting of needles pricked his trapped one.

As time ticked away, the cold snaked through his body like fog slowly creeping over the landscape until it was everywhere.

*Lord, I know I've been a stranger lately, but I need You. Gramps and Rachel say You are always with us. Help me get out of this.*

His teeth chattered, and he shivered. He needed to stay awake, but his eyelids drooped. Then his head dropped forward, hitting against the side of the ice-encased rocky surface. He didn't care. Maybe if he rested for a while…

Growls and yelps ricocheted through his tired mind. Jake jerked his head up and aimed the flashlight above.

Amber eyes stared down at him.

"Did you see that?" Rachel pointed to an area about three hundred yards in front of them and to the right. "I saw a light. It's gone now, but it was coming from the ground. That could be Jake."

"That's near those fissures in this meadow."

"He could have fallen into one."

"Let's go." Rachel charged out in front of Lawrence.

He grabbed her arm. "Wait. Look." He gestured toward the area they were heading to.

Rachel froze, her gaze riveted on a pack of four wolves, all standing around and peering down. At Jake? Hurt? "What do we do?"

Gramps handed her the flashlight and grabbed the rifle he'd slung over his shoulder before leaving the Jeep. "That's why I always come prepared."

"You're going to kill them?" Because she went hiking and camping, she knew how to use a gun, but one of the things she loved about her home was all the beautiful creatures that lived in Alaska.

"Not if I can help it. I had my fill of killing in the Vietnam War." His gruff voice softened and thickened when he mentioned being a soldier. Jake had once told her he would never talk about being in that war.

Lawrence crept forward. "Shine the light on them."

When Rachel did, a shot rang out in the night.

When the gunshot sounded, the wolves yelped, turning away from Jake, their attention on someone else. Had the assailant decided to see if Jake was hurt or dead? Had he brought reinforcements?

Sweat popped out on his forehead and rolled down his face. He was a sitting duck, but at least he still had some rounds in his weapon. He wouldn't go down without a fight.

Another blast echoed through the darkness, followed by a third one. Suddenly, the wolves jumped over the crevice and ran off, leaving Jake to face whoever was out there.

He lifted his Glock and prepared for the worst. With each second that passed, his heart rate increased until all he heard was its thundering beat against his skull. More sweat stung his eyes, and he blinked several times so he could see his assailant. He wouldn't have much time to make a decision. He pointed the barrel upward.

"Jake! Jake!"

Rachel's sweet voice, followed by Gramps's deeper one, took a few seconds to register and for him to drop his arm to his side. As he saw her peer over the edge, relief sagged his tensed shoulders, and he smiled.

*Thank You, Lord.*

Then his grandfather appeared next to Rachel. "You've gotten yourself into a predicament, son."

"Nothing you two can't handle, but before I turn into a block of ice, you might get some help. I'm going to have to be hauled out of here."

Three hours later, Jake lay on the couch in Linda's house while Rachel let the police chief out. Finally, some quiet after a very long and exhausting day. He closed his eyes, tired but not sleepy. He hurt, over his whole body, but he was too wired to get some rest.

When he heard Rachel's footsteps return from seeing Doc and Randall out, he shifted his head and looked at her—a welcome sight after the long evening he'd had. "I think we should ask Doc to move in since he's been here so much this past week."

Rachel laughed. "His wife might have a problem with that. Randall says he'll have the SUV towed into the garage and have it fixed, but it's going to take a while. Bodywork needs to be done as well as a windshield, not to mention the seat cushions with bullet holes in them. One only missed you by an inch."

"I wish you would leave Port Aurora until this case is solved," Jake said in a determined voice.

"I can't. I have to work through part of next

week, and I'm the best way into the fishery. You might not be able to snoop around, but I can. I have keys to most of the places."

Jake sat straight up, groaning as he swung his feet to the floor. "You will not do any investigating on your own. Do you understand?"

"Yes, I do."

A gleam in her eyes made him ask, "Do you understand and promise not to look into it by yourself?"

The corners of her mouth drooped. "I'm not answering that question."

"Rachel." Jake started to rise but sank back onto the cushion. "I can't be worrying about you while trying to figure out what's going on."

She lifted her chin a few inches. "And I can't be worrying about you, either. The assailant wasn't after me this time."

"Don't you think I know that? I'm going to call Chance O'Malley, my friend who is a state trooper, and ask him to come before Monday, if he can. The drug smugglers obviously are aware we're looking into the fishery."

Rachel sat on the coffee table near Jake while Linda and Gramps came into the living room. "Then use that fact to work against them."

Gramps covered the distance to the lounge

chair next to the couch. Linda poised on its arm and glanced at his grandfather. "Son, we overheard your conversation and think we have a plan that might help bring everything to a head."

Linda clasped Gramps's shoulder. "The problem is we need to figure out if it is drug smuggling or something else, and the only way to find that out is to get inside the shipping center and see what's going out. They will be processing two big catches tomorrow and Monday, then sending them to their destination on Tuesday and Wednesday. After that, most of the fishery will shut down for two weeks."

Gramps patted Linda's leg. "That doesn't leave a lot of time. I know all of us want this settled before Christmas. The alternative to not figuring out what's going on is to be a target for weeks and then try again after the first of the year. But then you have to return to Anchorage."

Jake slanted a look at Rachel, meeting her intense gaze. "Have you been talking to them while I was gone this evening?"

She smiled. "Maybe."

He frowned and turned his glare back on Gramps and Linda. "You are not police officers."

Rachel leaned forward, her apple scent swirling about him. "That's just it. But you are and can't investigate inside without an invitation or a good reason to be there. I work there, and Gramps is a concerned citizen, not an officer of the law. You need evidence to get a warrant."

"Right." Jake stood, anger sharpening his features into cold stone. "You and Linda are going to decorate for the fishery's annual Christmas party Sunday afternoon. While you're doing that, I'll walk on the pier again, and see how close I can get to those two boats that came in today. Also, I'll see what Chance has to say. If he can come earlier, he can walk with me."

"But you can't—"

"Rachel, that's it. I'm not going to put you in harm's way." Jake limped toward the hallway and escaped into the bathroom.

Leaning onto the counter, he took in the scrapes and bruises starting to appear on his face. He looked like he'd been in a fight and lost, but he wasn't giving up. His feelings toward Rachel were changing, and he wasn't sure what to do about them. But he did know that he wasn't going to let anything happen to her or the others.

* * *

Sunday afternoon, Rachel worked beside her aunt, setting up the tables and putting decorations on each one. Celeste was in charge of getting the large hall ready for the Christmas buffet and party. At one time they had been good friends, but ever since the incident with Jake, she had kept her distance from Rachel. She'd been so mad at Celeste at first that she didn't try to repair the rift, even after Jake left for Anchorage.

Celeste went all out for this event every year, and this one even more so. Once, Rachel had discovered Celeste made all the centerpieces for the tables throughout the year. She heard through the grapevine that Brad wouldn't let her work, and since they didn't have any children, what did she do all day? Their house on the hill was always beautiful and spotless, even when the fishery was going through hard times.

"I need to get a few more centerpieces. Be right back, Aunt Linda."

Rachel made her way to Celeste to see where the rest of the table decorations were. There were still six more to set up. Rachel waited until Celeste was finished talking with

Eva Cohen, who stormed away with a pursed mouth and a tic twitching in her cheek.

"What's wrong with Mrs. Cohen?" Rachel said when she approached Celeste.

"She can be so difficult. She is Brad's secretary, but you would think she runs the whole fishery with that attitude of hers. I don't know how my husband puts up with her."

"She definitely runs a tight ship. Maybe he should make her a captain of a boat, and she'd be gone most of the time."

Celeste chuckled. "Not a bad idea, but Brad raves about her, so I don't dare make that suggestion." She glanced toward Eva, who snatched up her coat and left the hall. "I'm glad Jake is okay after his wreck. He looked beat up this morning in church."

"That can happen when you fall into a fissure."

"When did he do that?"

"Friday night. When his car went off the road, he thought it would be faster to hike across the meadow not far from where we live."

"I remember when I used to pick wildflowers in that field with you…before Jake and I started dating. Is he still angry with me?"

"You need to ask him that." Before the conversation turned to a subject Rachel didn't want to discuss, she said, "I need six more centerpieces."

"I still have some in my car. Will you help me bring them in?"

"Sure. Let me get my coat. After my dunk in the harbor, it doesn't take much to get me cold."

"I was so sorry to hear that. Probably some drunk ran into you and didn't even realize what he'd done. Did Chief Quay ever find the guy?"

"No."

Celeste looked toward the main door. "Brad's here. I need to talk to him for a minute."

"Where's your car? I can get the centerpieces."

"Between the processing and shipping buildings."

Bundled in her warm coat, Rachel left the hall through the back door, which was closer to the shipping warehouse. She wasn't going to waste this opportunity to check it out. The only day of the week it was shut down was Sunday, so no one would be around. Her master key should get her inside. When she became part of management, she'd been given a set.

She glanced around for anyone watching her. The parking lot was deserted as well as the field that led to the water. Perfect time to see if she could get in. Then she could come back when it was dark. She'd even let Jake keep guard outside. At the door she inserted the key, then turned it. It didn't work. Why? It should. She examined the lock. It was new, not the weathered one she noticed a couple of weeks ago.

She started for Celeste's car, her step nearly faltering when she glimpsed Ivan coming toward her. Where had he been? She prayed he didn't see her trying to unlock the door. With a nod toward him, she cut across the parking lot, determined not to glance back at him. At Celeste's Lexus SUV, she opened the back door and reached for two of the centerpieces. When she pivoted to leave, she ran right into Ivan.

She started to say something, but no words came out. Why was he here? All she could focus on was the man's dark eyes, intense, narrowed on her. A movement behind him snagged Rachel's attention.

Rachel called out, "Celeste, I love your new car. I've seen you driving it around. It still has that new car smell."

"It drives great on snow." Celeste paused next to Ivan. "It's good to see you, Ivan. With your help, Rachel and I will only have to make one trip."

Rachel sidled toward the rear of the silver-gray SUV while Celeste retrieved two centerpieces from the backseat and gave them to Ivan without the man saying a word. By the time she picked up the last two, the man's expression evened out into a bland look.

As he strolled with them toward the large hall, he said, "I'm glad I can be of service to women in distress." Finally, he grinned at Celeste and held the door open for them to go inside first.

Rachel shivered. When Jake smiled, she always felt the caring and warmth behind it. When Ivan did, she felt a chill, although he would be considered a classically good-looking man, tall, with a muscular build and raven-colored hair and eyes.

After Ivan set the two centerpieces on an empty table, he left. Celeste watched him leave, her lips pinched together. "I don't like that man," she murmured.

"Before you arrived at your car, he seemed…" Rachel realized she shouldn't say any more. Celeste was married to the owner.

"He seemed intense?"

"Yes. I don't have a lot to do with him."

Mainly because Ivan usually sent his assistant with the shipping information and billing to Rachel's office. "Is he always like that?"

"Afraid so. Brad insists he's indispensable. But a lot of the workers give him a wide berth."

In the next hour, the hall was transformed into a winter wonderland of white, red and green. Rachel stood with her aunt on the perimeter and surveyed the decorations.

"Celeste is quite talented. The centerpieces of different Christmas scenes are fascinating. I found myself examining each one I put on a table." Aunt Linda swept her arm toward a round table on the edge at the back. "I want to sit there tonight. Celeste's creation reminds me of the time you, her and some other kids in Sunday school put on the nativity scene for the church."

"I remember that. Jake was Joseph. Celeste played Mary while I was the angel." Rachel fixed her gaze on the table across the room and near the rear door. "That does remind me of that."

"Are you two ready to head home?" Lawrence asked from behind them.

Rachel half turned. "Where are Jake and Mitch?"

"He's coming. He's walking Mitch down to

the loading dock, then circling the building." Lawrence threw a long glance toward Aunt Linda and winked at her.

"Isn't that being obvious, especially after what happened Friday night?" Rachel asked as her aunt's cheeks reddened.

"That's the great part about it. He met Brad in the parking lot, and they started talking about the expansion. They decided to tour the outside with Brad explaining what had happened and what will."

"That's odd. Brad and Jake were a couple of years apart and never that close."

"You know what I think? Brad feels threatened with Jake in town."

Aunt Linda shook her head. "Lawrence, where in the world did you come up with that?"

"I saw Jake and Celeste talking before church. So did Brad."

"They did?" Rachel searched the room to find Celeste. "I didn't know that." Why didn't Jake say anything? They used to share almost everything.

"We'd better go if we're going to turn around and come back in a couple of hours," Aunt Linda said as she grabbed her parka. Lawrence helped her into it.

At her Jeep, Rachel spied Brad and Jake

shake hands, and then he and Mitch made their way to her. "Did you discover anything interesting?"

"Nope, except that Brad's silent partner has deep pockets. Brad has all kinds of ideas for expanding the business and town. He has a point. The town is located between the sea and mountains. It's perfect to grow the recreational fishing, camping and hiking industry. I have a friend in Anchorage who owns a chain of sporting goods stores in Alaska. Josiah and his twin sister, Alex, are always looking for ways to expand. Alaska has something to offer that other states don't. It's the last frontier in the United States with parts still rugged and hard to get to."

Rachel slipped behind the steering wheel, started the Jeep to get it warm and waited for the other two to climb in. "If the town continues to grow like it has the past year, we'll need more than the general store and the few restaurants to cater to the townspeople and the tourists."

As she drove out of the parking lot, Brad and Celeste emerged from the meeting hall. The expressions on both their faces made Rachel wonder if they'd had a fight. Did Celeste tell Brad about Ivan?

When Rachel parked at her house, she grabbed Jake and held his arm to keep him inside the Jeep while Lawrence and Aunt Linda headed indoors. They took Mitch.

Jake assessed Rachel. "Did something happen today?"

"Why don't you tell me?"

"What?"

"Your grandfather said you had a conversation with Celeste before church. What did you two talk about?" She had no right to ask him that question, but she was the one who tried to help him piece his life together after Celeste broke off the engagement. She couldn't do it again.

"She was asking how I felt after the wreck on Friday."

There was curiosity in his tone. Staring out the windshield, she gritted her teeth to keep from saying anything. She wasn't going to force him to confide in her. If he wanted to get hurt again, then—

"But mostly we talked about what happened eight years ago. She actually apologized for what she did."

"What did you say?" *What did you do?*

"I told her in the end it was for the best. I just didn't know it at the time. Coming back here has made that clear to me. As we talked, I realized that I don't hold any grudges against her. That surprised me at first."

*Me, too.* But Rachel kept that to herself. "What's different?"

"I'm different. I'm not the same heartbroken guy who left for Anchorage. I should have come home years ago, and I would have realized Celeste and I wouldn't have worked."

"That's good because all I can say is you'd better not be a stranger to Port Aurora ever again. I missed you." The last word caught in her throat.

Jake edged closer and clasped her hand. "I've missed you, too. I don't know what's happening between us, but I want to see where it goes."

She touched his lips with her fingertips, wanting to say so much but settling on, "I like the idea of getting reacquainted with each other." She was falling in love with Jake—that was the only thing that explained the feelings she was having. But how would she know for sure? She'd never been in love—had purposely avoided it. Maybe she was wrong. Confused thoughts raced through her mind.

He stared at her for a long moment, then

released her hand as he put his on the car door handle. "Is everything set for tonight?"

"Yes. I'd hoped that you and I could check out the shipping warehouse tonight while everyone was partying, but I discovered that my master key no longer works. They've changed the locks."

Jake rotated toward her, thunder in his expression. "You did what?"

Rachel flinched at the fury in his voice. She needed to do something to help, but all Jake wanted to do was protect her.

# TEN

Rachel pressed back against the driver's-side door. "I didn't really plan to do it. I saw an opportunity while going to get the centerpieces from Celeste's car to try my key in the door. I looked around, and no one was there. I wasn't at the door more than half a minute."

Jake curled his hands and squeezed them so tight they ached. "What part of *don't investigate the building* do you not understand?"

"I wasn't going to. But if my key had worked, and it should have, I was going to suggest I go back with you and Mitch later tonight. I know you shouldn't search the warehouse without a warrant, but I can. I could take Mitch and see if he found anything. You could keep watch. Well, at least that had been my plan, until the key didn't work."

Her explanation flowed nonstop from her, which indicated to Jake she was nervous. She should be. "I don't think you grasp the seriousness of this situation."

"I've seen TV shows about—"

"Stop right there. Real life crimes aren't wrapped up in an hour or two with a happy ending. These people mean business. Chance talked with a DEA agent who said recently their office in Seattle has become alerted about Peter Rodin's recent activities."

"What activities?"

"His association to a big-time Russian mafia boss."

"Do you think because we are so close to Russia, someone at the fishery is smuggling in drugs from there?"

"It's at the top of my list of theories."

"I can't believe Brad would condone that."

He loved how she always looked at the good in people. She'd lived a sheltered life. Probably the first time crime touched her was Betty's murder. "He might not know. It's only recently that law-enforcement agencies discovered a link between Rodin and the Russian mafia. If I were going to look at boats involved, it would be the ones added after Rodin became a silent partner. Also, there are a lot of new employees since the expansion. Any number of them could be involved."

"So they could be using the fishery without Brad's knowledge?"

"Yes."

"Then we need to get Mitch onto the Alaskan King and maybe even the Tundra King since it was overhauled in Seattle."

"There could be a scent, but without the drugs actually on the boat, it would be hard to use that as evidence. They would move the drugs off the trawler as soon as possible."

"During unloading?"

Jake nodded. "Have any shipments gone out since the last boats came in?"

"Not until the first of next week."

"I'll need a list of the shipments. Where they're going. When. How." He hoped to turn this investigation over to Chance O'Malley and the DEA, so all he needed to do was protect Rachel, Linda and Gramps.

"I usually get the information after the fact for billing purposes."

"Who has it?"

"Ivan Verdin. His department readies the fish for shipping after processing, schedules the deliveries and moves them to the ship or plane."

"That's where the drugs will be, in shipping, then on some transport to their destination."

He spied Gramps standing at the front window by the Christmas tree, trying not to look at them in the Jeep. "We probably need to go in."

"I'll go see Ivan tomorrow about the shipments. I'll tell him I want to wrap everything up before vacation starts on Wednesday."

Jake's gut tightened. "No. Gramps, Chance and I will keep our surveillance on the shipment warehouse to find out when the shipments go out. I want you as far away from there as possible. You are not involved in this anymore."

"Are you going to be at the bait shop again?"

"No, I have a room for Chance at the bed-and-breakfast that has a great view of the harbor. He's flying in tomorrow morning. I'll pick him up at the airport and make a big deal that a friend is visiting. That will give us a reason for going in and out of his room."

"I'll stay away from shipping if you promise you'll be careful. Someone came after you on Friday, not me."

He held out his hand. "A deal."

She fit hers within his. "Yes. I want my town back."

He'd never forgive himself if something happened to her. She meant too much to him. She'd always been there for him, and he was the one who had let her down. He left rather than dealt with his feelings after Celeste called off the wedding. Then he poured his life into his work, focusing on helping others in his job and spare time. He never really came to terms with his mother leaving or Celeste breaking their engagement. He'd been running away from his feelings for years. Maybe that was why he felt so strongly about returning to Port Aurora.

"Jake, are you all right?"

He blinked, orienting himself to the present. He still held Rachel's hand, and in the dim light he saw worry lining her face. When neither of them was at risk, he needed to have a long talk with Rachel. He wanted to make sense out of all these feelings swirling around inside him.

"I don't know about you, but it's cold out here. Let's get inside before Gramps sends out a search party." He grinned, released her hand and opened the door.

When Jake entered Linda's house right behind Rachel, Gramps gave Rachel then Jake a mug of coffee. "I figure you need it to thaw out. I could have thought of warmer places to talk."

A blush tinted Rachel's cheeks as she made

her way to the fire. She put her drink on the mantel and held her hands out near the blaze, rubbing them together. "This feels good."

Linda came from the kitchen with a plate of cookies. "This can tide us over until dinner tonight. Celeste told me fish would *not* be on the menu. The main course will be prime rib."

Gramps patted his stomach. "What a treat! Although without fish to catch, Port Aurora would be an extremely small community."

Jake moved closer to the fire. What was going to happen to the town if the fishery was involved in drug smuggling? If Rodin was behind it, how would the fishery keep going without its major backer? Thousands of people would be affected if the main industry failed. If he had a hand in taking it down, Jake needed to figure out a solution.

Rachel scanned the crowd crammed into the huge hall at the fishery. This year the Christmas party had been opened to a lot more people besides the workers. In addition to the elaborate buffet tables featuring many side dishes, freshly baked bread, salads and desserts, she counted four different stations for prime rib, ham and chicken. At the front of the room stood a fifteen-foot Christmas tree, decorated in different fish ornaments interspersed among glittering balls of silver and gold.

"Brad and Celeste outdid themselves this year," Lawrence said over the noise in the hall.

Jake put his hand at the small of her back. "Speaking of Brad, I need to talk to him. He said something today about giving me a tour inside the fishery, and I'm going to see if he can tomorrow. Do you see him?"

Rachel leaned toward him and whispered, "I thought you were turning the investigation over to your friend tomorrow."

"I am, but I'll help where I can. Chance wouldn't likely get a tour of the shipping warehouse, but I can."

Rachel took Jake's hand and pulled him toward the right side of the room along the wall. "So it's okay if you keep putting yourself in danger, but not me." Jake was only involved because of her.

He inched close to her. "Yes. I'm a police officer. I've been trained for this. You haven't."

For years she'd worried about him in Anchorage, especially when she'd heard of a serious crime committed there. The serial bomber had heightened her fear something would happen to Jake. And it had. "You don't want me in danger. I don't want you to be, either."

"It's part of the job. Before I left for Anchorage, I was a police officer here, and you never said a word."

"Because crime here wasn't anything like a serial bomber, gangs, murder. With all that has happened, it just makes me realize how dangerous your job is."

He boxed her in, hands placed on the wall by the side of her face. "There's nowhere totally safe. Stay out of this."

She stared at his mouth, set in a firm line. "I'm going to, but what will happen if we can't get proof?"

"There is no more *we* in this investigation." He frowned. "But to answer your question, until that moment comes, let's think positive. When I was injured and had a lot of downtime in Anchorage, Jesse Hunt, another canine officer, kept me informed of what was going on for a while. I sank deeper into depression. I was stuck on medical leave and couldn't do a thing about a case, and yet it consumed me. About a month later something had to give. I needed to focus on my recovery, or the feeling of helplessness I was experiencing would grow. I've learned to concentrate on the moment—not the future."

She'd remembered how he had been when

he first came home and saw Celeste. "How about the past?"

He cocked one corner of his mouth. "I'm working on that. It helped to talk to Celeste this morning. But when you come home after being gone so long, the past hits you square in the face. I can forgive Celeste, but I don't know if..." He heaved a sigh.

"You can forgive your mother?"

"It's one thing to be rejected by Celeste and totally different by the woman who gave birth to you."

Rachel cupped his face. "I know, and you've had a constant reminder of that while you've been here. I'm surprised you put Chance in the bed-and-breakfast."

"It was the best solution. It isn't the same place as when I lived there as a child with my mother."

Chief Quay stepped into her peripheral vision, and all thought of continuing this conversation vanished.

"What are you two concocting?" the police chief said with a chuckle.

Without missing a beat, Jake replied, "She's trying to pry information about her gift from me."

"Yeah, I hate surprises." Rachel placed her

hand on Jake's arm. "Nobody is waiting to eat. If we don't get our food, there's not going to be any left for us."

"Leave it to Rachel to worry about dinner." Jake threaded his fingers through hers. "Any news about Friday night?"

"Nothing. The other set of footprints near the SUV went toward town for about two hundred yards, then crossed the road and went down a turnoff. There were tire tracks, most likely from a big truck. That must have been his transportation, but there are tons of trucks in Port Aurora. We're matching the tire tracks with a database, but what we've found doesn't narrow the hunt down much. Don't worry. I'll let you know if anything worthwhile comes up."

"Thanks, Randall."

Rachel watched the exchange between the men. Jake didn't feel the police chief was involved, but he couldn't rule him out, either. How entrenched was the drug-smuggling ring in the town? The thought that the police might be part of it nauseated her. For Jake it would be devastating. He knew some of the officers—worked with half of them. But she couldn't deny Aunt Betty's warning, either.

Jake panned the crowd, his gaze pausing on the other side of the room. "I see Brad is in line. Let's hurry and get behind him and Celeste. I want to finagle that tour out of him after I get Chance settled. It will be interesting to see if he says yes."

"What will you do if he says no?"

"Go to the next plan."

"And what's that?"

His roguish grin appeared, his dimples and bright eyes enthralling her. "I could say Plan B, but that's cliché, and I don't have a Plan B at this moment."

"You think you can charm a tour out of Brad?"

"No, but I could out of Celeste, especially after her apology this morning. She'll want to make amends."

Celeste might have apologized, but Rachel didn't want her escorting Jake anywhere.

He slung his arm over her shoulder and weaved their way through the throng of people until they arrived at the buffet tables set up on the left side. Jake walked down the line until he reached Brad, who was second from last.

Jake held out his hand. "This is some party you've thrown."

Brad pumped Jake's arm vigorously, then draped his arm over Celeste's shoulders as though staking claim to her. "You clean up nice."

Jake swept his arm down his body. "Oh, this old suit? I was told I needed to dress up or stay behind, then I heard there would be prime rib and I put on a tie. Not my favorite piece of clothing."

Brad laughed. "I know what you mean. Most days at the fishery it's informal. This town doesn't have too many reasons to dress up. Celeste wanted this to be one of them. We're having a DJ play music after dinner. Has your dancing improved over the years you were away?"

Jake looked him straight in the face. "Not one bit, so I won't be taking part in that activity."

Brad swiveled his attention to Rachel as the line moved forward. "Then if you need a partner, just come get me." He switched his gaze to Celeste. "That is, if my wife is okay with me dancing with another woman."

"Please do. After all the decorating today, I'm exhausted. I'm going to sit back and watch everyone." Celeste smiled at someone behind

Rachel. "Captain Martin, I heard you had a great catch."

The captain of the Sundance, a short man with a full black beard, paused. "I'm impressed with all you managed to do today. When I helped bring in the tables, I never thought the hall would be decorated so lavishly, Mrs. Howard."

"A hobby of mine to keep me busy."

"You've outdone last year," the Sundance's captain said, then continued to the back of the line.

"I have to agree, Celeste. You had to be working for months on these decorations." Rachel picked up her plate at the beginning of the long table. "Brad, I've been telling Jake all about the changes you're making. I wanted to show him around, but I have to get the next payroll out by Wednesday instead of Friday."

Jake squeezed Rachel's hand. "That's okay. Brad said something about giving me a tour when we talked earlier." He looked right at the owner. "Maybe you have some time tomorrow."

"Sure. I'd been thinking about it since we talked earlier. How about eleven thirty?"

"That's good." Jake filled his plate with potato casserole, green beans with almond slices, mandarin pasta salad and bread. To Rachel he asked, "Do you think carrying two big plates might be uncouth?"

Rachel nodded her head toward Brad. "You'll be in good company."

By the time they sat at the table Aunt Linda had saved for them, Rachel's stomach was rumbling loud enough that Jake chuckled. "You should have gotten a second plate."

She grinned at him. "That's okay. I'll go back for seconds, then you and I need to dance the calories off afterward."

"Weren't you listening? My ability to dance hasn't improved one bit from high school."

"It doesn't take a brain surgeon to figure out how to slow dance. You just rock back and forth to the music."

"If he doesn't, Rachel, I would be glad to," Gramps said as he cut a big piece of the prime rib and slid it into his mouth.

But hours later as the crowd dwindled to half the guests, Jake came up behind her chair, bent over and murmured, "If you still want to dance, I will."

She turned her head and peered over her shoulder, Jake's mouth inches from hers. She leaned back, her pulse racing. "You don't have to."

"No way am I going to let my grandfather put me to shame. Look at him dance." Jake gestured toward Lawrence and Aunt Linda on the floor with the other couples. "I must have inherited some of his genes." He held out his hand for her.

She took it and rose, and ten seconds later he whisked her into his arms and swept her out into the middle of the other dancers. "I thought you didn't know how to."

"I don't, but I've been watching. I'm a quick study."

When he suddenly dipped her and twirled her around, she stopped. "Who have you been watching?"

"Gramps, who else?"

"You might follow someone younger."

His forehead crunched, and he scanned the couples around them. "Oh, you mean like this." He dropped her hand he held out straight and clasped his arms around her middle, slowed his pace and began swaying. "Is this better?"

"Much," she said as she laid her head on his shoulder, the day's activities catching up with her, her heartbeat thumping against her rib cage. But in the midst of her possible assailants, she felt safe with Jake.

With his scent swirling around her, she

closed her eyes, imagining them alone—no drug smugglers, attempts on their lives or a murder victim. If only it were that way.

As Rachel stared out the window on the passenger's side of her Jeep, she wanted to dwell on last night when, for a short time, she could believe all was well with her world. But all she had to do was look at Jake's scrapes and bruises on his face to know otherwise.

Jake pulled in front of the fishery's headquarters and parked. Rachel turned toward him. The next couple of days would be the best chance to catch the drug smugglers as they sent out their last shipments of the year—at least they hoped they would. After the holidays, Jake would be gone, and she hated the idea of going to work and wondering who to trust at the fishery—or in town, for that matter. If Brad's silent partner in Seattle was behind this, the blow to Port Aurora could be devastating. But the town's revival shouldn't be from illegal activities.

"Remember, go about your duties and no more snooping. Gramps, Chance and I will take care of that. Okay?"

"Yes, I have a lot to do today. The checks go out two days early, but no one remembers to send me the paperwork I need. Also, since this is the end of the year, there's a lot to do with the books, information to track down." She started to get out, stopped and glanced at Jake, taking in his face she'd known for years but seeing so much more there than when they had been teenagers. "By the way, I poked around in the accounts and can't find any unusual amounts coming in or going out."

"Probably a second set of books to keep this from you."

She smiled, watching his expression, set in determination as if his mind was already on the task of catching the drug smugglers. "Be careful. I don't want to have to worry about you."

As she turned away, Jake clasped her arm and tugged her back to him. He laid his lips over hers and drew her as close to him as he could with a console in between them. The sensations she'd been trying to suppress came to the foreground. No other man ever made her feel as Jake did.

When he pulled back, he cupped her face, and his gaze locked with hers. "And I don't want to have to worry about you. We're gonna talk when things are settled down in Port Aurora."

The intensity in his voice sent flutters through her stomach. “About what?”

“Us.”

“About being friends?”

“No, we’re past that. I’m not sure where we’re headed, but I know I care more for you than just a friend.”

“You’re right, this is different. We aren’t the two teenagers who hung out together and were best friends.” She ran her finger across his lips, wishing they weren’t sitting in the parking lot of the fishery. “I guess I’d better go to work.” Although at the moment she didn’t want to leave the car.

“Stay safe.”

“I intend to. Only my duties, no extracurricular activities. I feel better with Chance O’Malley coming in this morning.”

“Yeah, while we’re at the airport, we’re going to take a look around. We’ll have to be quick so I can go on that tour with Brad.”

She opened the door. “Come see me after the tour. Maybe we can catch a late lunch.”

“Sounds good.”

The grin that spread across his face radiated charm, making her want to stay, to be with him, to discover everything that happened to him during their eight-year separation. When she was inside the building, she had a bounce to her step as she walked to her office. Then she spied the work on her desk, and reality came crashing down.

She hung her parka on the peg behind the door and locked her purse in her bottom drawer, then sat. All she wanted to do was think about Jake's kiss and the fact he wanted to talk about their relationship, but the ringing of the phone jolted her back to the present, and she answered it.

"This is Mrs. Cohen. I received a call from Captain Martin. He had an emergency and won't be able to run the time cards to you this morning. He said just go on his boat and into his cabin. They're on the table by his bunk."

"Is there something wrong?"

"He's taking his wife to the doctor. She was up all night sick." Even over the phone, Eva Cohen's formality and strict discipline came across in her tone.

"I will. Thanks for letting me know."

Brad's secretary hung up without saying goodbye or giving Rachel a chance to.

Before leaving for the harbor, she checked all the necessary paperwork she needed from each boat and wrote the few names of the ones who still hadn't sent theirs. She might as well go by each one and pick up what she needed if the captain was there. This was one of her biggest headaches—getting what she needed to do her job, especially with the growth in the number of boats the fishery utilized.

After bundling up because the wind was strong coming off the bay, Rachel strolled to the pier. Dawn was sneaking into the night sky with a few splashes of yellow and rose to the east. She hadn't heard if a storm was brewing out in the Bering Sea. That body of water could be treacherous, especially in the winter months, even without bad weather.

Her first stop was the Tundra King. She rang the bell the captain had posted on the dock to signal someone wanted to come aboard. When no one appeared on deck, she was tempted to climb onto the boat and take a look around. Then she remembered her promise to Jake and clanged the clapper against the bronze with more force.

She'd come by at the end and see if anyone was on the boat by then. She turned to leave when Captain Kirk Cohen came out of the wheelhouse.

"Sorry. I saw you and knew what you wanted. Here are the time sheets and catch info." The captain walked along the side of the trawler until he reached where she was on the dock and handed her the papers.

She nearly lost them in the exchange as the wind whipped between vessels. “Thanks.”

As she left, she nodded toward Beau Cohen and another member of the Tundra King’s crew as they passed her on the dock to hop on board. Before disappearing inside the boat, Beau winked at her, the gesture startling her. What was he up to?

She visited three more trawlers before she arrived at the Sundance, her last stop before returning to the warmth of her office. She went on board and made her way to the captain’s quarters on the deck level. His cabin was to the fore and through the galley and salon for the crew while at sea.

She knocked on the closed door in case Captain Martin was able to return to the boat earlier than he anticipated. When no one answered, she eased it open and stepped into his quarters with a view of the harbor out the bank of windows. The choppy water rocked the ninety-foot boat. The fishermen were used to walking in rough seas. She wasn’t. The papers she needed were right where Mrs. Cohen said they were. She walked from one piece of furniture to the next, scooped up the manila envelope with her name on it and started back toward the door.

Standing just inside, Beau and Captain Martin blocked her only means of escape. Danger emanated from both men from their clenched fists to their scowling faces.

# ELEVEN

In the reception area of the small building attached to a hangar at the Port Aurora Airport, Jake waited while Chance's plane landed. He was thankful it was able to land since the crosswinds were getting stronger. The twin-engine Cessna fought them and made it—barely. Jake released a long-held breath as the door opened and his friend exited.

Jake, with Mitch on a leash by his side, left the building to meet the state trooper partway. They shook hands, then hurried inside, stomping the snow off their boots.

"Glad you're here." Jake closed the door.

"I wasn't sure we were going to land. It was shaky, and I'm used to going to out-of-the-way places in Alaska." Chance leaned over and petted Mitch. "He's looking great. Retirement agrees with him." Chance slid Jake an assessing look. "How are you doing?"

"I'm managing. Although this trip back home hasn't been what I thought it would be." Jake pointed at his single duffel bag. "Any other luggage?"

"Nope. I brought only what was necessary."

Jake went to the counter, leaning against it. "Will you let us know if any planes will land or take off tomorrow? My friend, Chance O'Malley, may have to go back to Anchorage earlier than planned." He slipped her a card with his cell and the bed-and-breakfast's number.

The woman behind the counter smiled. "Yes. There's one scheduled tomorrow at ten, weather permitting. Mostly flying in supplies and taking a big shipment from the fishery, but he might be able to tag along as a passenger. There is another flight right before sundown, too, if he needs to leave later."

"How about Wednesday?"

"The same schedule as Tuesday."

"Thanks, Toni." Jake smiled at the lady, then headed for the door. "Let's go, Chance."

Outside, Jake quickened his pace to the Jeep parked at the side of the building. When they were both inside, he angled toward his friend. "I went to school with Toni, who runs this airport with her husband. I had no trouble looking around before you arrived. No shipments for the fishery in the hangar. The flight you were on is the only one today. It isn't taking back much cargo except letters and packages, although it did bring in the mail and some supplies for the general store. I think the drugs will be shipped tomorrow or Wednesday."

"How about by boat?"

"Gramps has paid the harbormaster a visit. They're friends. He thought he would play some dominoes with Charlie. They usually end up doing more talking than making moves." Jake drove toward town.

"So we're going to the harbor?"

"No, I'm taking you to the bed-and-breakfast. Your room has a great view of the buildings and the harbor. I thought we could use it for surveillance purposes. The owner of Port Aurora Fishery is giving me a tour at eleven thirty. I want to see what's going on in the shipping warehouse. I think the drugs are probably going from the boats to there." Jake withdrew a diagram of the harbor and buildings and handed it to Chance. "Then I'll be back, and we all can have lunch and talk strategy."

"Sounds good. I might take a walk to familiarize myself with the town."

"I should be back around one, and you'll get to meet my friend, Rachel."

"The lady that started all of this?"

Jake laughed. "Yep. Gramps is supposed to head here when he's through pumping his friend for information."

Jake left Chance at the bed-and-breakfast and hurried across the street and toward the harbor. He was to meet Brad at his office. Inside, he decided to stop by Rachel's first and tell her Chance made it.

As he approached the open door, he remembered the night before. She felt right in his arms as they slow danced. For a while all he thought about was her—not the drugs, attempts on them or Betty's murder. Then at the end, when everyone lit a candle and the lights went out in the hall, he held her hand as they sang "Silent Night." In that moment he missed being home. He missed being with Rachel more. His life in Anchorage wouldn't be the same unless he could persuade Rachel to move there.

When he stepped into the doorway, he opened his mouth to say hi, but the empty office mocked him. Where was she? He walked in and looked around. Her coat was gone. For a few seconds concern nibbled at him. Then he remembered all she said she had to do.

He wrote her a brief note about lunch and stuck it on her computer screen, then went in search of Brad.

When he met Mrs. Cohen, Brad's secretary, he immediately understood Rachel's misgivings about the woman. An iceberg might be warmer than that lady. She stood when he came in and looked at him out the lower part of her glasses. He didn't let her demeanor stop him from saying, "I'm here to see Mr. Howard."

"Does he have an appointment with you?"

"Yes, eleven thirty. Jake Nichols." Mitch, standing beside him, made a low growl. Jake stroked him, but his dog remained tense though quiet.

A brief frown descended, directed at Mitch, before she replaced it with her haughty look. "I'll let him know."

He decided to rattle her. "That's okay. I can." With Mitch next to him, Jake strode toward the door and thrust it open.

Mrs. Cohen charged past him into Brad's office. "I—I… He says he has an appointment with you, but I don't have it down."

Brad waved his hand. “Sorry. I forgot to tell you. We made it last night at the party.”

She heaved a deep breath, then spun on her heel and left.

Jake started to make a comment, but Brad held his palm up and he mouthed the word, “Wait.”

Brad pushed back his chair and said, “I’m eager to show you all that has been done this year,” then grabbed his overcoat and shrugged into it. “We’ll start with the plans I have for an additional processing center.”

Jake wanted to steer him to shipping, but if Brad was involved in the drug smuggling, he didn’t want to be too obvious. It bothered him that a friend he’d known as a child could be caught up in the illegal activities, but Brad had always had rich tastes, so it really wouldn’t surprise him if he was having financial problems.

When Jake reached the hall, remnants of the Christmas party had been cleaned up, except the tables and chairs. “If I didn’t know better, I wouldn’t believe such a wonderful celebration went on last night in this place.”

“That’s Celeste. She put it on and made sure it was taken care of this morning. She loves doing stuff like that.” He swept his arm to indicate the large area. "Some men are going to come in late this afternoon and remove the tables and chairs, and then this will be one big empty room. Celeste is a great organizer."

As Brad talked about Celeste, his comments didn't bother Jake. His feelings for Celeste were gone. During the party as he watched her move among the guests, decked out in an expensive red dress, not a hair out of place, he realized her leaving him before they were to be married was the best thing in the long run. He'd been dazzled by her beauty, and although she was gracious and kind to the townspeople, she always held herself apart as though she were playing a role. He didn't think he'd really known the person behind the facade.

Whereas with Rachel, he used to be able to predict her next move. She knew him better than even Gramps when they were growing up. Everything she was thinking was right there in the open. No guessing. A person knew where he stood with Rachel.

"Everyone enjoyed themselves, and the prime rib was a big hit." Jake also didn't hold a grudge against Brad because he moved in on Celeste when she was engaged. Letting go of the anger freed him. Now he understood what Gramps and Rachel had said about forgiveness. Being mad at Brad and Celeste really only hurt him in the long run. He was the one who stayed away from Port Aurora and let any relationship he had with Rachel dwindle to almost nothing.

Brad stopped in the middle of the cavernous room and slowly rotated all the way around. "I need to talk to you without people seeing or listening."

His hushed tones drew Jake's full attention and Brad's action, rubbing his palms together, looking from side to side, held Jake's concentration. He slipped his hand into his parka and grasped his gun. Had Brad lured him here to kill him? Every nerve ending sharpened its awareness.

Finally, as though satisfied they were alone, Brad stepped closer and expelled a deep breath. "Some strange things have been going on at the fishery. I think Ivan is doing something illegal behind my back. On Sunday I was going to go into shipping and do some checking, but the lock had been changed. I didn't authorize that."

"Did you ask him about the new lock?" Jake held up his hand for a few seconds while he stuck his other hand into the top shirt pocket and showed Brad he was recording their conversation using his cell phone.

Brad gave him a slight nod. "Yes. He said he just did it and had forgotten to tell me. He would have a new key for me this week."

"What was wrong with the old one?"

"Nothing. But it was old and could be picked easily according to Ivan."

"Is that true?"

Brad combed his fingers through his hair. "I guess so. Up until Betty's murder, serious crimes didn't happen in Port Aurora. I suppose I've let security go lax because our town has been relatively untouched by crime, especially in the winter months." He sighed. "But with the expansion, more people are coming to Port Aurora, and crime is increasing."

Was Brad playing him? Was he really innocent of the drug smuggling? "What do you think is going on?"

"It's got to be some kind of smuggling. Maybe drugs. I don't know. I've looked at Rachel's accounting, and everything seems on the up and up, but have you ever had a gut feeling something is wrong and it is?"

"Yes. I've learned to trust my gut. Who do you think is working with Ivan? If he's smuggling something in, he has to have coconspirators. Where is he getting the drugs from, if it is drugs?"

"That's why I'm talking to you. I don't know. There are parts of this fishery I don't have access to. I'm the owner. I've always gone freely anywhere around my company. Now doors are locked in buildings and to buildings."

"What doors in which buildings?"

"I went into shipping this morning to talk to Ivan, and then I walked around. One freezer was locked and a small storage room."

"What did Ivan say about that?" Jake asked, studying Brad for any signs of lying.

"Nothing. I couldn't find him."

Still not sure if he could trust Brad, Jake asked, "What do you want me to do?"

"You're a police officer."

"Not here in town."

"Okay, I don't know if I can trust ours. Ivan and Officer Steve Bates are good friends. I've seen them hanging out together at night."

Jake thought back to Friday night and recalled seeing Bates come into the Harbor Bar and Grill and sit at the bar. Ivan sat next to him for part of the night before the officer left. They talked occasionally during that time but also to others. That fit with what Betty said to Rachel about not trusting anyone.

"What do you want to do?" Jake wasn't going to say anything about a state police officer staying at the bed-and-breakfast until he felt Brad wasn't playing him.

"Contact some people you trust. I'll give them permission to search the whole fishery. If there isn't a problem, then I've overreacted, but I'll be relieved that the company is doing only legal business."

"Let's go, then." Jake started for the exit.

The sound of a shot cracked the air.

Rachel gulped and backed up against the table. As she gripped its edge, strength flowed from her legs, but somehow she managed to keep herself upright as Beau came toward her and Captain Martin shut the door.

She fought the fear attacking every part of her. Beau was muscular and huge. *Is he the one who hit Aunt Betty so hard she died?* Trembling followed the fear and encompassed her whole body.

Beau gripped her upper arms and jerked her toward the bunk nearby. After he shoved her down, he took out a rope and yanked her hands together, then bound them in front of her. When he produced a second length of rough twine, he knelt, removed her boots and tied her ankles together so tight she didn't think blood would circulate to her feet.

"Too bad you had to be so nosy. Now we have a mess to clean up," Captain Martin said, still standing by the exit.

"I came in to get the payroll papers," she said in a quavering voice. "As Mrs. Cohen told me."

"Don't take us for fools." Beau stepped back from the bunk.

"Just ask her."

"I know she did because I told her to. It's all the other snooping you've been doing." Captain Martin glared at her.

"What are you going to do with me?"

"Why, kill you, my dear. Didn't you get the message that snoops end up dead like Betty?" The captain shook his head and put his hand on the door handle. "You don't cross the Russian mafia."

As Captain Martin left, Rachel peered at Beau. "I don't know anything."

"We know a state trooper flew in this morning. That ain't a coincidence."

"I don't know a state trooper."

Beau backed away from the bunk, his cackles sending goose bumps down her body. "You might not but your boyfriend does. Don't worry, he'll get his due soon enough."

"You don't need to kill me. Use me as a hostage."

His hideous laughter filled the cabin. "We don't need you. When the rest of the crew is here, we're putting out to sea. When we're far enough out, I'm going to kill you, then dump your body over. The current will take you where no one will find you. Frankly, after the fish take care of you, you won't be recognizable. You know it might be fun just to toss you into the water alive and let nature take its course."

As Beau turned toward the door, Rachel sent a prayer to God. *I need Your help. Anything is possible through You.* There was still time that Jake could save her.

"Oh, just in case you think your boyfriend is going to come to your rescue, he won't. He's being taken care of as well as the state trooper. Then people in Port Aurora will learn who really runs the town." Beau slammed the door as he left, the lock clicking into place.

Leaving Rachel alone.

Devastated.

Hopeless.

* * *

A bullet whizzed by Jake and struck Brad, who cried out. As he collapsed to the floor, Jake dropped down and knocked a metal table onto its side to use as a shield, rolling it to also protect Brad. The shooter was behind a concrete pillar about fifteen yards away.

Mitch jerked on his leash, wanting to do what he had for years. Jake couldn't risk him, even though his K-9's heart was in it. He pointed to Brad and said to Mitch in a low voice, "Lie down. Stay." When his dog was stretched out beside Brad, guarding him, Jake asked his friend, "Where are you hit?" as he cased out their chances of getting out alive.

Brad moaned. "Ch—est."

Another shot blasted and splintered the corner of the table by Jake's head, a fragment piercing his cheek. He hoped the assailant was counting on Jake being unarmed since he was on vacation. He contemplated returning fire but wanted to see if the man would do something foolish like rush him.

He peeked around the table and saw a man dressed in a black ski mask dart to the next pillar. Jake still didn't shoot when the assailant came out from behind that protection and raced to the nearest concrete support, forcing

Jake to roll the table to the side to shelter Brad, Mitch and him.

Minutes ticked away with only silence from the shooter. Was he playing his own mind game? Jake sneaked a look and noticed a door behind where the assailant was. Did he escape? Would he be coming in another door to take him by surprise?

He needed to know. Jake popped up, taunting the guy to shoot him.

Nothing.

Jake had to get medical help for Brad—fast. He took out his cell and called Randall. Although not totally sure how involved the police were in the drug-smuggling ring, it was a risk he had to take. He needed assistance, or Brad would bleed out. The red splotch on his coat was growing quickly.

"Randall, this is Jake. I'm at the hall at the fishery where the party was last night. Someone shot Brad, and he's bleeding a lot. The shooter may or may not still be here. He was behind the third support pillar from the back on the left side."

"Be there."

They needed more protection in case the assailant had escaped and was coming in another door. Jake placed the table where he could rush to the next one and lift it onto its side to be a second shield. He dragged Brad closer to the back exit with Mitch moving beside the fishery owner. As Jake upturned a third table, the shooter leaned out from the pillar and fired several rounds at them. The last bullet grazed his arm. He winced. Ignoring the pain, he focused totally on what he had to do to get them out alive.

This time Jake shot back, and the guy ducked behind the concrete support. After positioning the third table, Jake pulled Brad even closer to the door. Adrenaline pumping, Jake was deciding if he should go for a fourth one when the door on the assailant's side burst open, and the police chief and an officer rushed into the building. While they pinned the shooter down, Jake tugged Brad to the back exit with Mitch beside them. Brad had passed out, and Jake prayed the one ambulance in town was there.

His arm throbbing, Jake opened the door and used his leg to hold it ajar while he hauled Brad the rest of the way out of the building. When Jake straightened, an officer ran toward him, gesturing at the ambulance speeding into the parking lot. The two paramedics jumped out, and one hurried to Brad while the other retrieved the gurney from the back.

Once the paramedics took over, Jake said to Mitch, "Stay," then headed toward the door, intending to help the police inside.

The officer stopped him. "You're hurt. You need to go with the paramedics, too."

Jake glanced at his arm, blood on his coat sleeve, but nothing like Brad's. "Not until I'm sure Randall is all right. Who is with him?"

"Officer Bates."

When the engine started on the Sundance, Rachel knew her time was ticking down quickly. Once they were away from the harbor and out of sight of land, she would be killed and tossed into the sea. If she didn't die from the bullet, the frigid water would kill her.

The boat began moving. Rachel wiggled off the bunk until she could stand up. She looked out the bank of windows at the front of the trawler. She wasn't giving up. If she could get to the window, maybe somehow she could signal for help. The only way was to hop the ten feet.

Slowly, she jumped toward the windows, but when she was only two feet away, the trawler picked up speed close to the mouth of the harbor. The sudden jerk forward sent her to the floor, her left shoulder slamming into the wooden planks, her head bouncing up then down.

Pain radiated from her arm. She rolled onto her back and stared up at the ceiling as the boat accelerated even more. *I was too late.* The thought taunted her with despair.

*No, you aren't going to win. I'm in God's hands. He's with me.*

She pushed herself to a sitting position and scanned the cabin for any kind of tool to help her untie herself. Once freed she would find a weapon to use. She wasn't going down without a fight.

Using her knees to bear her weight, she bridged the distance to the bunk and plopped her tied hands onto it to assist her up. When she straightened to a stand, she scanned the cabin for anything to help her untie her hands. All she saw was a glass in a holder on the desk. She inched along the bunk toward it, steadying herself when the boat pitched. Her stomach roiled like the waves did. Fighting the nausea, she reached the edge of the desk and used it to move down its length.

The Sundance veered to the right, and Rachel flung herself across the desktop to keep herself upright. Sucking in shallow breaths, she tried to calm her racing heartbeat. The glass was inches away. She rolled partway on her side and reached for it. Her fingertips grasped the lip of the drinking cup and she lifted it from its holder, barely clutched between her two hands, the coarse rope chafing her wrists.

Her chest burned with lack of adequate oxygen. Again the trawler lurched, this time to the left. Rachel slid to the floor, the back of her head hitting the leg of the desk. She heard the glass hit the wooden floor and shatter. For a few seconds she closed her eyes, the nausea rising into her throat.

*Lord, I need You.*

Slowly, she opened her eyes to the swaying room. She found the shards of glass and plucked up the largest one to slice her ropes. Back and forth she maneuvered the jagged piece, occasionally its sharp edge slashing into her wrist. The blood flowing from the wounds made it harder to hold the slippery piece of glass, but she couldn't stop.

They were going to kill her if she didn't do something. As she repeated that over and over, she kept working on cutting the ropes about her hands while listening for anyone approaching.

Then the sound of footsteps echoed the warning one of the thugs was coming for her.

Were they already far enough from land to kill her? Frantically, she sawed the last part of the twine binding her hands. It fell away, and she hurriedly went to work on the ropes around her ankles. The door handle rattled as though a key were being inserted.

His Glock in his grip, Jake eased the back door into the hall open and used the rolled tables to sneak forward. The sound of a gunshot reverberated through the cold air. Peeping around his barrier, he assessed the situation, needing to know where the police chief, Officer Bates and the man in the ski mask were. Jake glimpsed Bates coming into the room from the side door near the rear while Randall stood at the far end. In between lay a still body with a black ski mask on, probably shot by the police chief. Bates hurried to the downed perpetrator and felt his pulse.

"Is he alive?" Randall walked toward the shooter on the floor and his officer.

Bates took the gun on the concrete and rose. "Yes." Then he lifted the assailant's gun and aimed it toward the police chief. Randall halted, his eyes widening.

Jake stood and squeezed off a shot a second before Bates did. The blast resounded through the hall as Randall dove to the left and Bates collapsed to the floor, the gun skidding across the concrete. Jake rushed him as the officer fumbled for his gun holstered at his side.

He made it to Bates a few steps ahead of the police chief. "Don't force me to shoot again." Jake pointed his Glock at the officer's head.

The ski-masked man on the floor groaned and tried to get up. Randall pushed him down, then rolled him over and removed his black covering. Sean's eyes glared up at the police chief, then connected with Jake's.

Although Jake had told Rachel he suspected everyone until proven innocent, seeing Sean lying on the floor stunned him. Jake felt like he'd been punched in the gut, all air rushing from his lungs. He clenched his jaws together so tightly that pain streaked down his neck.

Sean looked away. "You're gonna regret this," Sean said through gritted teeth as he clutched the side of his stomach, blood leaking through his fingers.

"I'll call the ambulance to come back for these two and have your officer Clark come in to help you. Then I've got to make sure Rachel, Gramps and Chance are okay. Chance is a state police officer who can assist you in searching the shipping warehouse and processing center." Jake kept his voice low so no one could overhear him. He was still concerned. Where was Ivan?

Randall frowned. "Why didn't you let me know he was coming?"

Jake pointedly looked at Officer Bates. "I wasn't sure who to trust." He hurried toward the back door, hoping that Officer Clark was nearby.

The police chief called out, "I've got another man coming. He was on a call outside town."

As Jake exited the building, the ambulance pulled away with Officer Clark coming toward him. "I need you to call the ambulance back as soon as Brad is dropped off."

"I heard gunshots, but Chief asked me to stay with Brad until he was safely away from here. Who's hurt?"

"Sean O'Hara and Bates." Jake refused to acknowledge Bates as part of law enforcement.

Officer Clark tensed. "Is Chief Quay all right? How bad is Bates?"

Jake signaled Mitch to come to him. "Randall is okay, and Bates was hit in the left thigh. He'll survive and go to jail." The police chief needed help. Jake hoped the rest weren't on the payroll of the drug-smuggling ring.

"What do you mean?" A scowl grooved deep lines in Clark's forehead.

"He tried to kill Chief Quay. I'll let him explain it. How is Brad?"

"The paramedics said it was a through and through in his shoulder. He should be all right once he gets to the clinic."

"Good. I've got to find Rachel."

Jake took off in a jog toward the fishery headquarters, hoping she was back in her office. When he reached her office, the vacant room goaded him into searching the whole building. No one he saw knew where Rachel was. Jake, with Mitch beside him, ended his hunt at Brad's office.

His secretary rose when he came into the room. "May I help you?"

"Have you seen Rachel? It's urgent."

"No. I haven't talked with her this morning."

"Any suggestions where she could be?"

"She could be anywhere. She flits from one place to the next." Disapproval dripped from the secretary's words.

"Thanks." He started to turn away when he heard Mrs. Cohen pull a drawer open. He stopped and swung back as the older woman raised a gun.

* * *

As the lock clicked open, Rachel dove across the bunk for the nearest weapon she could see, binoculars, which she gripped while she scrambled to hide behind the door.

When Captain Martin came into the cabin, Rachel used all her strength and brought the improvised weapon down on the back of his head. For a couple of seconds, he remained standing, and Rachel started to hit him again, but he crumbled to the floor. She quickly closed the door and then checked to see if he was alive. Blood oozed from his wound.

The only rope not cut up was the one around her ankles. She took it and brought his hands behind his back and tied him up. Then she spied a smelly rag and stuffed it into his mouth. She searched his pockets for the key to the cabin, found it and grabbed her boots. After slipping them on and snatching her coat from a chair, she hurried to the door and peeked out into the short hallway. Clear.

Without another thought, she quickly left, locking the cabin, then hurrying to the end of the corridor. If she could get to the life raft on the side of the trawler without being seen, she hoped she could lower it to the water and somehow escape. It was that or remain and be killed. It wasn't the best plan, but she didn't even know if Jake thought she was missing. She would take her chances with the Bering Sea. The water felt calmer than before, but when she emerged outside, she still saw white-caps from the waves.

She snuck toward the life raft in its white container on the side, keeping an eye on the door to the wheelhouse, where Beau and who-ever else was on board probably were. She'd seen a demonstration once a year ago and prayed she remembered how to do it. With one line tied to the railing, she tossed the can-ister overboard, and when it hit the water, she jerked the painter line two times to inflate the life raft. As it filled with air, Rachel had to wait a couple of minutes, the whole time scan-ning her surroundings.

From inside she heard a shout. Did someone see her out here? She had to jump now even though the raft wasn't quite blown up. More loud voices came from the wheelhouse, and the door began to open. Her heartbeat thunder-ing in her ears, she leaped over the side, hop-ing she hit her mark, rather than the ice-cold water. The second she landed in the life raft, she untied the rope and looked up.

Beau poked his head over the railing, saw her

and pulled his gun from his waist. She ducked inside the covered boat as a shot rang out.

"Don't," Jake said in a tight voice over the sound of Mitch's growls, his Glock aimed at Mrs. Cohen's chest. "I won't hesitate to use this if I have to."

Her arm stopped in midlift, anger hardening her features.

No doubt Mrs. Cohen heard the gunshots at the fishery. "So you are involved in the drug-smuggling ring." Every muscle in Jake locked, ready to react at the slightest movement from the woman.

She pressed her lips together.

"Put the gun down and walk from behind the desk." Jake took several steps toward her. "Mitch might have only three legs, but he can attack. He can still perform his police dog duties."

Her narrowed gaze stabbing into Jake, Mrs. Cohen slowly laid the gun down, then skirted the desk.

He stood behind the older woman, wishing he had a set of handcuffs. "Mitch, guard." Then he urged Mrs. Cohen forward. "Where's Rachel?"

"I don't know what you're talking about. I

have no idea what you think I'm guilty of, but I have a permit to carry that gun. I was defending myself against a man waving a gun at me."

He ground his teeth to keep from replying. Outside, he headed with Mrs. Cohen toward Randall talking to two of his officers near the shipping warehouse.

The police chief saw him and came toward him. "What happened?"

Before Jake could answer Randall, Mrs. Cohen said, "I want this man arrested for pulling a gun on me."

"She's involved, possibly the ringleader. She refuses to tell me where Rachel is, and I don't have time to wait for her to smarten up."

"I'll take her from here. Can I use Mitch in the shipping warehouse? We haven't found Ivan, but while my men are searching for him, I want to see if your dog can detect where the drugs are."

"Brad gave his okay to search the whole fishery, although in this case you don't need it since we were ambushed." Jake passed his K-9's leash to the police chief and gave a signal for Mitch to go with Randall. Then Jake headed for the bed-and-breakfast. He needed help finding Rachel and prayed he was overreacting.

When he reached the house and walked

down the hallway toward Chance's room, a cold lump in the pit of his stomach spread its icy fingers. He entered and came to a halt, standing over a prone body, gagged and bound on the floor. Gramps sat on the bed with his rifle pointed at the stocky, unfamiliar man. Hatred in his blue eyes drilled into his grandfather, then shifted to Jake.

Before he could find out what happened, the door to the bathroom opened and Chance came out, sporting the beginnings of a black eye. "You'll have to fill me in later. Have either of you seen Rachel in the past hour leaving the fishery headquarters?"

Gramps shook his head.

"What's she wearing?" Chance asked.

"A powder-blue parka with fur around the hood. Black pants and boots. She's about five feet five."

"I saw a woman of that description heading for the pier about forty minutes ago. She stopped at a boat, and a man handed her a manila envelope, then she moved on to another one."

"That was the time I was at the café grabbing coffee for us while we staked out the shipping warehouse. I didn't see her, son."

"Brad and I were ambushed in the hall by

Sean. Officer Bates tried to shoot Chief Quay. Obviously, this one was sent to take care of you two."

"There was another—Ivan Verdin. He got away and is sporting a limp." Gramps frowned. "I ain't as spry as I used to be, or he would be hogtied like this one." He shoved to his feet. "Let's go find Rachel while you tell me the details about your ambush."

"I'll take this one to a police cruiser, then check in with Chief Quay and let him know about Ivan. I've already called in reinforcements." Chance hoisted the captured assailant to his feet.

Jake followed his grandfather to the door, paused in the doorway and said to Chance, "Brad gave his permission to search the fishery, and the police chief is using Mitch to help him."

Then he left. As they approached the port facilities overlooking the harbor, Jake told Gramps about the shootout in the hall.

Charlie grinned when he saw Gramps coming inside. "You just can't stay away. Once a fisherman always..." His voice trailed off into silence as he took in their serious expressions. "I'm pretty isolated over here. Were you two involved in the commotion at the fishery?"

"Yes, we're looking for Rachel Hart. Have you seen her lately at the pier?" Jake asked.

"About thirty minutes ago."

"Where?" Jake's gut solidified into a hard knot.

"She was going on the Sundance."

*Why?* "Did you see her get off or go anywhere else?"

"She went by several boats. She does that a few times a week."

"Which boats?"

Charlie rubbed his nape. "Let's see. The Alaskan King was one." He snapped his fingers. "And the Tundra King as well as Bering's Folly."

Jake walked to the large glass plate window that overlooked the harbor from the right side, opposite the fishery. "I see the Alaskan King and Bering's Folly in port. Were the Tundra King and Sundance going back out?"

Charlie's thick gray eyebrows slashed together. "I've been in the back eating lunch so I didn't see them leaving. They weren't supposed to be. Tundra King was delivering a shipment to Seattle but not until tomorrow." He crossed the harbormaster's office and stood next to Jake.

Jake pivoted toward Gramps. "I'm going to

the pier to see if anyone has seen Rachel. I don't have a good feeling about this, especially with someone going after Brad."

Gramps frowned. "Why did they try to kill Brad?"

"Because he knew something was going on and wanted my help."

"Son, I'm coming with you."

"Gramps, you have to go back to Chance and have him alert the Coast Guard. They need to check those boats and hunt for Ivan. I hope that Chance can get Sean, Bates or the other thug to talk." Jake strode to the door and left.

He quickened his pace toward the pier. Seeing the flags flapping in the wind, he realized its force had died down. He hoped the storm forming had diminished. Jake started with the first boat and worked his way toward where Tundra King and Sundance were moored. Either no one was around or they saw Rachel coming to the docks but didn't see her leave. The wind didn't have to blow to send a chill down his spine. One of those boats took Rachel out to sea.

He couldn't shake that thought as he approached the Blue Runner and stepped on board. "Tom, are you here?" he called out when he opened the back door that led into the living quarters.

The captain came out of the galley, took one look at Jake's face and said, "I thought I heard gunshots. What happened? I was just grabbing a cup of coffee. Want any?"

"No, have you seen Rachel this morning?"

"Sure. She stopped by and checked to see how I was doing about an hour ago. Why?"

"She's missing. Why was she down at the docks?"

Tom sipped his coffee and looked out the window. "Getting time sheets and paperwork for payroll. I turned mine in. Others don't always. It's been a frustration for her, especially the new captains."

"Did you see where she went after talking to you?"

"Yeah, the Tundra King."

A tightness constricted Jake's chest. "Did she go on board?"

"No, she rang the bell the captain set up for visitors. Finally, he came out and gave her a manila envelope. Then she went to the Sundance, the dock over." Tom pointed in the right direction.

"Did you see her leave the Sundance?"

"No, but I wasn't watching all the time. I was working on a maintenance schedule."

"Did you see either boat leave the harbor?" All he could drag into his lungs were shallow breaths as his heart rate increased.

"The Tundra King. Suddenly, the crew appeared not long after Rachel had left and prepared to go to sea."

"But you didn't see the Sundance leave?"

"They must have in the last fifteen or twenty minutes while I was getting coffee and a sandwich."

"Thanks."

After Jake hopped off the Blue Runner, he hurried to the other dock, examining the wooden planks for a sign of what happened to Rachel. But there wasn't anything out of the ordinary. He stopped by each boat on that dock, but there was only one fisherman around, and he never saw Rachel get off the Sundance, but again he said he wasn't watching for it so she could have.

Enough wasted time. He hoped that Chance had alerted the Coast Guard, stationed at Port Aurora, by now because he didn't think Rachel had much time left. Their cutter was the best boat to go after the Sundance, especially with its head start. Jake prayed that Rachel was alive when they caught up with the boat.

# TWELVE

Huddled beneath the canopy, Rachel sent up yet another prayer. More gunshots sounded, several striking her life raft. But the waves were carrying her farther away from the trawler. She peered around the opening and saw Beau hurrying toward the wheelhouse, no doubt to come after her while a Sundance crewman continued firing at her.

She ducked back under the canopy and moved from the opening. As she crawled away, a bullet struck the raft on the side near her. She heard the hissing of air leaking out.

Jake gripped the railing on the Coast Guard cutter at sea, heading toward the Sundance. The boat had been spotted. *Is she still alive? Or what if I have it wrong, and she's on the Tundra King?* A second Coast Guard ship had been dispatched from another station and would intercept the trawler on its course toward Seattle. But if she was on that boat, it could be too late by then.

Chance came up beside him. “Everything is set to stop the Tundra King.”

“That’s good.” The icy wind whipped at him, but Jake wouldn’t go inside. He could see the Sundance in the distance and had been praying that they would rescue Rachel in time.

“We’re making good time. I was told the Coast Guard would board first, then we could.”

“What if they tossed her overboard before we get there?”

“There are spotters keeping an eye on the vessel. Smuggling is one thing. Murder is a bigger crime. Let’s hope they decide to take the lesser of the charges.”

Jake half turned toward his friend. “I’m a cop. I want to be at the front of the assault.”

“Not your jurisdiction, but we wouldn’t be here if it weren’t for you.”

“Still, we might not be in time. We don’t even know if we have the right boat.”

Chance clasped his shoulder. “We will. We’re due a break.”

Jake stayed at the railing while Chance went inside to go over the boarding with the crew.

Little by little the cutter shrank the distance between them and the Sundance.

When the Coast Guard was near enough, the captain of the cutter announced over a PA system, "Halt. Prepare to be boarded."

The Sundance increased its speed. The cutter followed suit, and the captain again demanded they stop. When they didn't, the Coast Guard fired a warning shot near the vessel. Finally, the Sundance slowed and then stopped.

As the boarding party jumped onto the trawler, Jake waited until the last man had, then he and Chance hopped on to the boat, following behind the Coast Guard crew. The sound of a blast cracked the air, and everyone dropped behind cover. More gunfire rained down on them. They weren't going to give up easily.

Jake was close to the side that led to the wheelhouse, while three shooters were at the back of the main cabin. He signaled to Chance to cover him while he ran forward, hoping he could come in behind the kidnappers. As the boat rocked back and forth in the increasing wind and waves, Jake raced toward the wheelhouse, low running past the side windows of the salon. He peeped into the wheelhouse. Empty.

When he eased the door open and snuck inside, he half expected someone to jump out. But it was clear. He headed for the galley and eating area between the wheelhouse and the main cabin. As he crept forward into the dining space, Beau popped up from behind the counter in the galley and fired at the same time Jake did, then dived into a nook that partially hid him. He immediately flattened himself against the wall as a crashing sound reverberated through the air.

Adrenaline pounding through him, he stole a quick glance into the galley. Jake spied an arm flung out on the floor, as though Beau had been hit and had gone down. He thought he might have hit him, but being cautious, he rushed forward, alert, his nerves on edge. When he found Beau down, he felt for a pulse. He was alive, but with a bleeding wound in his left shoulder. As Jake moved around him, he switched his attention between Beau and the main cabin.

There was a loud volley of gunshots, another thump to the floor, then someone shouted from the cabin, "I surrender."

While the four kidnappers were rounded up, Jake and Chance searched the boat, going down below to check the two cabins before coming to the captain's. When Jake burst into the room, he hoped to find Rachel. Instead, Captain Martin lay on the floor, moaning behind a rag stuffed in his mouth.

While Chance checked the injured man, Jake moved to the bunk and picked up the pieces of cut rope. Anger swelled in Jake, and he threw them back on the mattress. She had to be here.

"He's coming around. I'll take care of him while you continue looking for Rachel." Chance pulled out his handcuffs.

As Jake began to leave, the captain murmured, "She's not here."

"I won't believe that until I search every inch of this vessel. She's here. I know it." *She has to be, Lord.*

The inside of the boat had been covered so he went aft to inspect the containers they put their catch in. As Jake passed through the salon where the Coast Guard had the two men handcuffed and a medic treating Beau, it was all Jake could do not to grab him and beat Rachel's location out of him. What if she had already been thrown overboard before they even spotted them?

Outside by the back of the boat, he flipped the lid on the first insulated box. Nothing. The second one was the same, but when he lifted the third top he found fish. Strange. He started to move on to the next container, stopped and went back to the last one. He plunged his arm into the box, his fingers grazing a metal bottom. Only the fish.

Straightening, he looked around. What was he missing?

The head of the boarding party joined Jake. "Did you find your lady friend?"

Rachel was more than that, but he might never have a chance to tell her how important she was to him. No, he wasn't giving up. "No. Chance and I looked everywhere. Any idea?"

"I'll have a couple of my men look around, too, while we interrogate the crew."

Jake trailed the lieutenant into the salon, glancing back at the sky starting to darken. Night would fall soon, which would make finding Rachel even harder.

The lieutenant conferred with one of his men guarding the three crew members, then he returned to Jake. "They haven't said anything, but he thinks the tall one at the end might say something. He looked afraid while the others were cocky."

"Then let's talk to them separately. We can start with that tall—"

"Lieutenant, the life raft is missing."

Jake watched the tall crew member's reaction. Flinching, he ducked his head and stared at his lap.

Jake lowered his voice and said, "I think the tall guy knows something."

"Then let's see what he has to say."

Jake and the lieutenant escorted the tall crewman to the wheelhouse. Before the guy could sit, Jake was in his face. "Where is Rachel? In the life raft?"

The crew member looked down at his feet.

"Do you know how serious the trouble you are in? Kidnapping. Attempted murder. Drug smuggling. If she dies, murder. You will never get out of prison. I'll personally see to that." Jake paused and drew in a fortifying breath. "The first person who helps will get a deal."

The tall guy raised his head and stared at Jake. "Yes, the lady got into the life raft, but Beau shot at it and hit it several times. It has to be losing air."

"Was she injured?" It took all Jake's willpower to refrain from grabbing the man's shirt and yanking him close and shaking him.

The guy shrugged.

Jake started to come at the tall crewman, but the lieutenant grasped his arm and kept him still. “We’ll find her. I’ll call for a helicopter to help us look. It’ll be dark soon and that will make it harder.”

Jake left out the side where the life raft would have been stored and gazed out to sea, rough whitecaps everywhere. Was she shot and in pain? Was the raft intact?

*Where are you, Rachel? I need you.*

Freezing, Rachel peered out the opening in the protective canopy. The sun neared the horizon to the west. She looked around to see if she saw the Sundance or any boat. Nothing but the waves, which carried her farther away from the trawler, getting rougher and bigger.

Hugging her arms to her chest, she sat near the opening, the wind pushing the life raft—toward land or farther out to sea? What did she know about the life raft? The ones the company bought were double-tubed and had an Emergency Position Indicating Radio Beacon. But the Sundance wasn’t part of the company’s fleet. Did it have an emergency system? She crept around the six-person raft looking for the EPIRB. When she found it, relief swept through her. She pulled it from its bracket and flipped the switch, praying a rescue vessel reached her before the Sundance did. And before her raft was compromised by the bullet holes in it.

She huddled away from the opening with a flashlight she grabbed near the EPIRB to use when she needed it. Shivers attacked her body like when she'd been pushed into the ice-cold water. Panic quickly followed.

*God, anything is possible through You. Please send rescuers—send Jake. I have so much I need to say to him.*

Slowly, her rapid heartbeat calmed as she thought of the Lord watching over her. As she thought of Jake. She'd loved him for years but hadn't realized the depth of her feelings. Could she bear a long-distance relationship?

As all light vanished, the waves attacked the life raft, tossing it about even with the ballasts on the bottom of the craft to keep it as steady as possible. She crawled toward the opening and glanced out. The raft was perched at the top of a large wave, then plunged down, icy water splashing into her face.

Back on the cutter, Jake paced as the Coast Guard tried to figure out the best place to look for the raft. The three wounded kidnappers were being treated. Chance was with some Coast Guard crewmen, guarding the kidnappers.

Darkness finally set in and increased the danger Rachel faced. If only he were with her…

The commander of the cutter approached Jake in the pilothouse. "An emergency signal was received from a beacon in our general location. We are headed toward it and hope that it's from the raft. My XO is talking to the captain of the vessel to see if they had an EPIRB on the life raft. A helicopter is also heading toward the coordinates from the beacon."

"Do you have a pair of infrared binoculars I could use? I'd like to go on deck and search. I've got to do something."

"I understand." He gave him the pair around his neck. "Take this. It's getting rougher, especially the farther away from land we go."

Jake descended to the lower deck, gripping the railing with one hand while holding the binoculars with the other. The wind cut right through him, even when he was heavily clothed. Was Rachel? Again he sent up a prayer for her to be rescued in time. The Bering Sea could be treacherous.

As he scanned the vast darkness beyond the cutter, he felt as though he were looking for a white rabbit in a sea of snow. He'd been in search and rescues where they were too late to save the person. He couldn't be this time.

A yell went up toward the front. A crewman spotted something in the water. As he hurried toward the coast guarder, his heartbeat slammed against his rib cage, his breathing shallow gasps.

"Did you find her?" Jake shouted over the roar of the wind and sea. "Where?"

The man pointed to the southwest while relaying the news to his CO. Jake scoured the area and saw a small raft raise to the top of a wave, then disappear down the other side.

"What's next?" Jake asked the crewman who started for the back.

"We'll launch our rescue boat at the back when we get nearer. We're closer than the helicopter."

At the back Jake turned to the XO and said, "I'd like to go with them. She needs to see a familiar face after all that has happened. Please." He threw in the last sentences because he couldn't have the man tell him no.

"You'll have to gear up and stay out of the way of the crewmen."

"I'll do anything you say." *Just be alive, Rachel.*

Five minutes later Jake climbed into the craft

that launched from the rear of the cutter. They bounced over the choppy sea toward the life raft. Using the infrared binoculars, Jake kept his eye on it, hoping to see Rachel. Nothing.

What if she wasn't on the raft?

What if she'd been tossed into the rough sea?

Those questions flittered through his mind as they came up beside the raft. A crewman jumped onto the raft through the opening in the canopy.

An eternity passed before he emerged, carrying Rachel. As he gave her to another crewman, Jake made his way toward them.

The man saw Jake and handed him Rachel, her parka soaking wet. In the dim lights from the boat, he looked into her face, her teeth chattering, her eyes barely opened. Hypothermia was setting in again, but at least she was alive and in his arms.

# THIRTEEN

Jake held Rachel against his chest while she slept. The paramedic on the Coast Guard cutter checked her out and said she would be fine. Hypothermia hadn't gotten a good grip on her yet. He kept the blankets covering her even when she stirred and pushed them off.

Chance poked his head into the room. "We're nearing the harbor. How's she doing?"

"Getting restless. That's got to be a good sign. Did any of them talk?"

"Not a word. But I think I can crack Captain Martin."

Jake clenched his jaws together, pain radiating down his neck. He hadn't been able to keep her out of harm's way. That was his job: to protect.

"She's safe. Don't beat yourself up over this. As a police officer you know you can't always anticipate every scenario. I'll be back when we dock."

With Rachel in his arms, at least safe now, he leaned back against the wall and closed his eyes. *Thank You, Lord. You protected her. I don't know what I would have done if she had died.*

Her eyelashes fluttered.

"Rachel," he whispered, stroking her face.

She nestled closer, cushioning her cheek against his shoulder. Her eyes opened and locked with his. "I'm so tired."

He held her tighter, never wanting to let her go.

"I think every inch of me hurts. I feel like I was put in a dryer and it was turned on high."

He grinned. "Are you telling me you are hot?"

"No, but I've been bounced around so much, bruises must be covering me."

He combed his fingers through her still-wet hair. "But you're alive. That's the most important thing right now."

"Did we catch the drug-smuggling ring?"

"Didn't I tell you that there is no *we* in this?"

She tried to sit up, but he didn't want to let her go. "I didn't go looking for trouble. I was sent to the Sundance on the pretext of my job. I think Mrs. Cohen is in on the drug ring."

"And she is in custody. She pulled a gun on me. I was faster."

"Is everyone in custody?" Worry coated each word.

He assisted her until they both sat on the bunk, their backs against the wall. He grasped her hand between them. "Don't know. It'll probably be a crazy few days when we get back. And until the whole smuggling ring is rounded up, you are not safe."

Rachel stared out the window as the sun came up on Wednesday morning. In thirty-six hours so much had changed. The drug smugglers were being arrested. If all went well today, Jake and Lawrence would return to their house for the rest of the time that Jake would be here. The thought saddened her. She'd loved having Jake back in Port Aurora. If he hadn't been here, she'd probably be dead right now.

A shudder zipped down her body when she remembered the men who would have thrown her into the Bering Sea to disappear forever. She'd seen the concrete block and chain they were going to use to weigh her down so there was no chance she'd be found.

All yesterday Jake and Chance had been investigating into who else had been in the drug-smuggling ring. Lawrence and a police officer had been guarding her when Jake wasn't there. They've not had any time really alone, and there was something she wanted to find out.

She'd missed Jake being around but understood why he wanted to be involved in the criminals being rounded up. He wanted to make sure she was safe before he left. Then they needed to talk. She just wasn't sure what she should say. She loved him, but she didn't want to live in Anchorage. It was bad enough being a police officer in a small town, but in a city like Anchorage, would she ever see him? He had admitted his work was his life, and because of that, she couldn't take him away from it.

She saw Jake walking with Mitch across the yard after visiting his grandfather's house. They were both expected in town at the police station before she went to work later. Brad had insisted she take Wednesday off, too. Her employer would be recovering at home himself for a few days. But she had the payroll to get out. The people who worked for the Port Aurora Fishery were depending on those checks, especially with it being right before Christmas.

Jake noticed her and waved. She smiled and watched him trudge through the new snow that fell the night before. It left a pristine white blanket over the terrain and reminded her how the Lord could change anything—the landscape, a bad situation into a good one, people's hearts.

As Jake stomped up the steps to the porch, Rachel made her way into the arctic entryway. He came into the house, shaking off the snow that clung to his clothes. Mitch did the same, then wanted her attention while Jake hung up his coat.

"I'm not sure why I'm even bothering. We need to leave for town soon. There's been a change in plan—they want you there for the meeting with the DEA. They also want you in the room when I interrogate Captain Martin. Do you think you can handle that?"

Rachel swallowed hard and nodded. She'd do anything that would help put this case to rest.

"Where are Gramps and Linda?"

"In the kitchen playing dominoes."

"When did they start that?"

"About a year ago. Lawrence taught Aunt Linda how to play dominoes, and she showed him how to play chess. He has yet to win a game, though."

Jake grinned. "So that's why he's been reading that book about chess. Are they going into town with us?"

"No. Lawrence wants to go cut down a tree for Christmas. She's going with him since he helped us with ours."

"When he came for the holidays in Anchorage, by the second day I'd come home from work to find a tree standing in my living room, ready to decorate."

"You wouldn't have it otherwise, I'm sure."

"Nope. If Gramps hadn't been there, I would have worked extra to give some of the guys with families time off during Christmas. I've never taken longer than a week for a vacation, so these past few months have been hard on me."

"And the last couple of weeks?"

"I have mixed feelings about that time. It was good to return to Port Aurora, and I can't say that I've been idle much. Of course, nearly dying isn't a great way to spend a holiday. But if I hadn't been here, I hate to think of what could have happened to you and Linda."

Visions of the burning house paraded across Rachel's mind. "It all started because Aunt

Betty asked for help. It's mind-boggling to think how one incident had such a rippling effect."

Jake covered the small space between them and clasped her arms. "We're going to the police station, but when we leave, I'd like to put the drug-smuggling ring behind us at least for the last two weeks of my vacation. Randall and Chance have been interviewing the employees of the fishery while I covered every inch of it with Mitch. They think they have everyone. A couple of them are talking."

"Yes, let's wrap this up so you can actually have a vacation, and I'll stop looking over my shoulder."

"I like that."

She relished his hands rubbing up and down her upper arms as though trying to warm her. "The new year is going to bring a lot of changes around town, but I want to wait until then to worry about what will happen to the fishery now that we know about the involvement with the Russian mafia."

"I told you about my friends who own Outdoor Alaska. This afternoon we're going to talk about opening a store here and investing in the fishery. Brad approved the meeting."

"I'm going to refill my coffee, then I'm

ready to go." Rachel walked into the kitchen as Lawrence pulled out the chessboard. "We're leaving. Do you need anything from town?"

He shook his head while her aunt said, "Lawrence says he needs more ornaments for his tree."

"I'll have Jake pick some out at the general store."

"I personally don't want him leaving your side until you are assured by Chief Quay everyone has been rounded up." Lawrence set his pieces up. "And I'm going on record that I think we should stay until we know one hundred percent you two will be all right."

"Know one hundred percent we're safe? That will never be, Lawrence. You know that. There comes a time we simply have to put our trust in the Lord." Aunt Linda moved a pawn.

He harrumphed as he stared at the board.

Rachel hurried and filled her travel mug, then escaped before they started arguing. Lawrence knew how independent her aunt was, but it frustrated him because he'd been good friends with her aunt's husband. He once told Aunt Linda that it was his duty to watch out for them. He made a promise to her husband. But it was much more than that. Rachel was sure he loved her aunt, but she wouldn't marry again.

"Let's get out of here before the fighting starts over the game." Rachel headed for the arctic entry. "My aunt threatened him the last time with bringing out her timer."

"That's the way he is with dominoes. He carefully considers every move and its consequences."

"Not really a bad trait." Rachel donned her heavy coat, gloves and hat, then tossed the keys to Jake. "You drive. I'm going to enjoy this coffee."

On the ride to town, Rachel brought up a subject she'd wondered about since he had returned. "Are you happy in Anchorage? With your job?"

"Why are you asking?"

"With Officer Bates arrested, there will be an opening at the Port Aurora Police Department. I know we don't have the same type of crime as in—"

"With the past couple of weeks, that has changed."

"And it will continue to as more people come to live here. I don't know what will happen with the fishery, but the business was successful this past year. The drug money didn't go to pay people's salaries. It went to fatten a few criminals' pockets. The expansion was needed to compete with other ports and fisheries. Everything has been done except the additional processing center." Rachel rubbed her sweaty palms on her jeans. "Chief Quay will be retiring in a few years. You could take over his job easily. I know he would recommend you to the city council."

He slowed and glanced at her. "Why do you want me to stay?"

"Lawrence is lonely. He has missed you. I've missed you."

Jake stopped in the middle of the road leading into town. "You have?"

"Well, of course. I think that's obvious the last couple of weeks. We've picked right up where we left off."

"Not exactly. We're eight years older. A lot has happened in that time."

Rachel thought about her life, and up until recently, it had been the same old thing. "Speak for yourself. You had a near-death experience a few months ago."

"And you don't call getting trapped in a burning house a near-death experience? Or being hauled out to sea to be dumped?"

"Those things just happened. It hasn't shaped me yet. Your experiences have changed you, as well as your job. Again, I'm asking you, are you happy in Anchorage?" She held her breath, waiting for his answer. She wanted to tell him how she really felt, that she loved him, but didn't want to pressure him. He had to want to stay, or it wouldn't work.

"I have my job, my friends and I volunteer with Northern Frontier Search and Rescue, which has been fulfilling." Jake resumed the drive to town.

"We have our share of search and rescues here, especially during tourist season. The big, bad world has intruded on Port Aurora. I want someone like you protecting this town." That was the last she would say about it. He had to make up his own mind.

He pulled into a parking space in front of the police station. "I will think about it. I always wanted to make a difference in people's lives."

"I'd say you've accomplished that in a short time here. You don't have to be in a big city to do that. I didn't like the feeling we couldn't go to the police." She opened the door. "People trust you. I trust you." She climbed from the Jeep and walked toward the police station, aware Jake was probably trying to understand why she brought up the subject.

Inside the building, people were crammed into the small space, which only had one interview room and the chief of police's office. Otherwise, it was open with a counter in front where the dispatch answered the phones and questions from anyone who walked in. The jail was at the back of the building. Officer Clark talked with a DEA agent while Chief Quay signaled for them to join him in his office with Chance and another man.

She peered back at Jake. "We've stirred up a hornet's nest."

"I have a feeling the three cells are full. I see two DEA agents are here."

"The only agency we're missing is the FBI."

"They're coming, but Chance is taking the lead on this case for the state. The FBI and DEA agencies are working together to round up Peter Rodin and his employees in Seattle." Jake reached around and pushed the swinging half door open.

When she entered the police chief's office, enough chairs for everyone filled the whole room. She squeezed over to the far one by the wall, figuring she wouldn't have much role in this meeting other than to answer a few questions. Jake sat in the one beside her and took her hand for a moment while his gaze captured hers. Through this whole ordeal, he'd been there for her. She couldn't have asked for more.

Chief Quay took his chair behind his desk and said, "I wanted to review what we've done so far and make sure all the loose ends are tied up. I don't want one of these people to get away because something wasn't done right. They came into my town and nearly destroyed it. We have never had a shootout in the middle of town, let alone murder, multiple assaults and kidnapping in such a short space of time. Jake, I understand you have worked with DEA agent Daniel Porter before."

"Yes. I'm glad to see you here representing the DEA. The lady sitting beside me is Rachel Hart, the one responsible for uncovering this drug-smuggling ring." Jake squeezed her hand, then leaned forward. "Who has been arrested?"

"The crews of the Sundance and Tundra King as well as their captains. Along with them, we also have Ivan Verdin and four other coworkers from the shipping department, Sean O'Hara and Eva Cohen." Chief Quay scowled. "And then there is my officer, Steve Bates. He kept them informed about anything going on with the police and Coast Guard, since his girlfriend was a yeoman at the station here."

"We are checking financial records for each person, especially in connection to Peter Rodin. As we follow the money trail, it's leading us to him," Daniel said, remaining standing by the door. "I believe Captain Martin will help us on this end once you talk to him, Miss Hart."

"We'll be transporting the suspects to Anchorage, where the facilities are more secure. Several more state troopers are coming in on a special plane tomorrow and will take them back. We're working with the DEA to see if this drug-smuggling ring has any other operations in Alaska. Our preliminary findings are leading to the conclusion this was a test run. Peter Rodin hasn't invested in any other businesses in the state." Chance shot a glance at the DEA agent. "I'll be here for the next week helping the DEA comb every inch of the fishery, but there are no financial records indicating Brad Howard is involved. It appears that Eva Cohen ran the operation as his secretary, controlling what he saw or heard."

Rachel thought of her last contact with the woman. "She's the one who sent me to the Sundance. She called and said Captain Martin had left all the papers I needed on his boat."

The police chief relaxed back in his chair.

"The injured assailants have been airlifted to the hospital in Anchorage. They will be under guard until they are released to be transported to jail. Are there any questions?"

"Will the fishery be able to open after the first of the year?" Rachel hated seeing the town suffer for a few greedy people.

"I've told Brad Howard probably or shortly after that. The investigation will have to be completed before life can go back to normal. The owner realizes he will be under scrutiny from the Coast Guard, DEA and the state for a while." Daniel put his hand on the knob. "Unless you need me, I'm going to take another crack at Verdin's second-in-command."

Chance rose from his seat, turning toward Jake. "We'll bring in a few dogs to check all the boats. They should be here shortly. Give Mitch an extra treat for all his work."

"I will."

After both Chance and Daniel left, Jake shook hands with Chief Quay. "Thanks for keeping us informed. Do you think it's safe now for Rachel?"

"Yes, but if that changes, I'll let you know. Go enjoy your Christmas vacation. You deserve it, Jake, and if you ever decide to come back to Port Aurora, there's a job for you here. If the drug-smuggling ring had gotten its hooks into the town any more than this, I hate to think of the crime rate. This is a good reason to keep the police staffed adequately."

As Rachel followed Jake toward the door, she threw a smile at the police chief. "Thanks."

"Officer Clark is bringing Captain Martin to the interview room. Anything he tells you about the smuggling ring will make our case stronger."

"I'll try."

As they left the police chief's office, Jake escorted her to the interview room. "I'll be with you, and he'll be handcuffed to the table. You'll be safe."

As she entered and her gaze fell on Captain Martin, she hadn't realized how hard this would be. She'd known him for years. Most of the people in the drug-smuggling ring were new to Port Aurora. So why did the captain take part in the illegal activities? He was going to stand by and watch her be murdered. The thought shivered through her. But she sat across from the man, trying to forgive him as the Lord wanted her to do.

"Why did you do this?" Rachel asked, needing to make some sense from all that had happened.

"First, thank you for agreeing to talk to me. I got caught…" Tears glistened in the captain's eyes.

She still ached, and her wrists and ankles were chafed red from the ropes. Jake had stitches in his arm from where he'd been grazed by a bullet. And this man had been in the middle of it all. "Why did you do it?"

Captain Martin cleared his throat. "My son lives in Seattle and owes this group a hundred thousand dollars. If I didn't help them, they'd have killed him and his family."

"A hundred thousand dollars? How?"

"Trying to keep his business solvent, he got in over his head with the wrong people."

"Where are your son and his family?"

"In hiding with the US Marshals. I wouldn't talk to you until they did that."

"What boats were working for them?"

The captain frowned. "The Tundra King is all I know of. We took turns meeting the Russian trawler with the drugs. I can give the authorities all that information."

"So everyone in your crew is involved?"

With sadness in his blue eyes, Captain Martin nodded. "I will testify. I'll do anything they want, but first I needed to ask for your forgiveness, Rachel. I never meant for someone I knew to be hurt. That tough show on the boat was for Beau Cohen's benefit. I don't know if I could have let them kill you and throw you overboard. I was coming to see you to talk to you. To see if there was a way to get you out of the situation alive. I deserved what you did."

Jake covered her hand in her lap. She slanted a glance at him and knew when they left she had to tell him she loved him, no matter where Jake ended up living. If Captain Martin had gone to the authorities when he was first contacted, this might never have happened in Port Aurora. But he held the truth inside him. She wouldn't anymore.

"I forgive you," she finally murmured, meaning every word. She shoved her chair back and rose. "Now, I need to get to the fishery, so the employees will be paid today."

As she left, Jake put his arm around her, and they walked side by side to the exit. She didn't say anything until they reached the fishery headquarters. "Are you coming in?"

"Yes. I'm still not one hundred percent sure you're safe, so I'm sticking with you until I'm satisfied."

"I like the sound of that. Let's go to my office."

When she arrived there, she hung up her

coat and took Jake's to do the same. Then she shut the door and turned toward him, the words she wanted to say to him on the tip of her tongue.

He pulled her to him. "Alone, finally. I've wanted to talk to you ever since you were found, but so much had to be wrapped up, and I had to make sure it was done correctly." He plastered her against him, his arms locking around her. "When I didn't know if you were alive or not, I knew without a shadow of doubt that you've always been the woman for me. We got so hung up on being friends that we suppressed our growing attraction for each other when we were teens. I love you. I want to marry you."

She laid her cheek against his shoulder, nestling into the crook of his arm. "Good thing we're smart as adults."

"Are you saying you'll accept my proposal?"

"You're right. I've been in love with you for years but kept denying it. I didn't want to be like my mother going from one man to the next. All I had was time to think while I waited on that boat, praying you knew where I was. But you found me, and deep in my heart I knew you would. We're connected—two halves of a whole. How can I deny my other half? I would be denying myself. I love you, Jake, and if you want to live in Anchorage…" Emotions swelled into her throat. She never wanted to leave, but she would for Jake. After swallowing hard, she continued. "I will make it work. But I'm warning you, I'll want to come back to Port Aurora *a lot*."

He brushed his lips across hers. Once. Twice before he pressed his mouth against hers in a deep kiss that spoke of his love for her.

# EPILOGUE

Christmas morning, a knock sounded at Aunt Linda's house in Port Aurora. Rachel hurried to answer it because her aunt was still asleep. They had attended a late-night service with Lawrence and Jake, and none of them had gone to sleep until two in the morning. She peered outside and saw Jake on the porch. It wasn't even eight yet.

She answered the door, throwing her arms around him and kissing him before he was even inside. "I've missed you."

"Soon, we'll be married, and I won't have to go home."

She stepped to the side and let him in. "I'm glad they have rounded up everyone in the ring including Peter Rodin, but I did like the fact you had to be with me all the time. I kinda got used to it."

After hanging up his coat, he backed her

into the living room and pushed her gently onto the couch, then settled next to her. "I know what you mean. That's why I want to marry you as soon as possible."

"So do I. I wish Aunt Betty could be here to see us. Who do you think killed Betty?"

"What little evidence there was indicates that Sean did. The other with him was Ivan. Their size and tread of a pair of their shoes match what was taken at the scene, and there was one set of latent prints in the pantry. That matches Sean's."

She really hadn't known Sean, but she couldn't say that about Jake. Over the years, they had been through so much. "Now I want to put it behind us. I don't want to talk about the smuggling ring. At least for today."

"Sounds fine to me. I came early because I wanted to give you my Christmas present alone."

"Where is it?"

He rose and walked into the arctic entry. When he returned a few seconds later, he had a wrapped box in his hand. "I hope you like it."

She tore into the red-foiled paper and removed the lid to reveal a Port Aurora police badge. She stared at it for a few seconds, then lifted her gaze to his. “Does this mean you’re going to work for them and we’ll live here?”

He nodded. “Working with Randall these past weeks, I realized this was a good compromise. My job will be different, but I can still use Mitch. Brad wants me to go through the fishery at random times to make sure there are no more drugs. The police department is going to apply for a grant for a trained K-9, and if we get it, I’ll be its handler. Josiah mentioned doing that when he met with Brad this week about being a partner in the fishery.”

“Do we know if he and his sister are going to invest in the fishery?”

Jake grinned. “I’m supposed to keep this a secret until the first of January.”

The twinkle gleaming in his eyes told her everything she needed to know. “They are! I could kiss you.”

“Go right ahead. I won’t complain.”

She held his head between her hands and planted her lips on his. “Thank you, Jake. I know you had a lot to do with it.”

“Not really. What Brad did expanding the fishery was on the right track, but you can’t tell your aunt anything.”

“I won’t. I’ll go make us some coffee. When

is Lawrence coming over?" She started to rise, but Jake grabbed her arm.

"In two hours. Didn't you forget something?"

"What?"

"My present."

"Oh, about that." She gave him a quick kiss, then stood. "You'll have to wait until after Christmas. I'm taking back the gift I had for you."

Jake arched an eyebrow. "Why?"

She retrieved a flat box from under the tree. "You'll see."

He carefully unwrapped it and peeked inside, then started laughing. "I guess I see why. These Anchorage employment applications won't be needed now, but I appreciate the gesture."

"I meant it. I would move to Anchorage if that was the only way we could be together. I don't want to be separated ever again."

He tugged her to him and whispered against her lips, "Nothing is going to stop us from being together."

* * * * *

Dear Reader,

*Standoff at Christmas* is the fourth in my Alaskan Search and Rescue Series. In this story Jake is a K-9 police officer who nearly died in the third book of this series, *The Protector's Mission*. I couldn't leave Jake's story alone after leaving him and Mitch, his K-9 dog, severely injured when they were searching a bomb site for survivors.

Jake had to have his own story and a happy ending, but I wanted to take him away from Anchorage and put him in an environment where he was vulnerable—his hometown. Not only did he have to recover from a life-threatening injury, he had to deal with his past. Jake couldn't forgive his fiancée for breaking it off to marry another man but also his mother for abandoning him.

This is a story of forgiveness, something the Lord wants us to do. It isn't easy, but once we do, it frees us from the bonds of the past. Carrying hate in our hearts only hurts us, not the other person. God knows forgiving another is freeing and gives us back our life. He only wants the best for us.

I love hearing from readers. You can contact

me at margaretdaley@gmail.com or at P.O. Box 2074, Tulsa, OK 74101. You can also learn more about my books at http://www.margaretdaley.com. I have a newsletter that you can sign up for on my website.

Best wishes,

Margaret Daley